T0365670

Reviews

David Dorris uses his awesome imagination in this awesome book, The Adventures of Stunning Stephen Edwards and the Stunning Kid! It's an awesome book with a lot of twist, once you start reading it, it is real hard to put it down!! It is a smart and fun book, I love how it goes back and forth with the modern day world and the Wildwest!!! I highly recommend it, especially if you are a western fan!

Stephen Edwards
Professional boxer

Author, David Dorris, has written a dreamy story that many readers may have experienced with the theme of helping their loved ones.

This story begins with Rex, Stunning Stephen Edwards and The West Side Kids, all from Davenport, Iowa, receiving the call to once again reduce bullies with criminal intentions. The Dean Dickerson gang wants to control by means outside of the law land and water ways for their personal gain.

The call for help comes from Rex's great, great, great grandfather in the Wild West time period in Dodge City.

How The Stunning Stephen Edwards and The West Side Kids answer the call for help is a fun experience for the readers. Comedy is always present when Scooter is involved in detective challenges. The ending is a surprise, too.

I would recommend this fun, light reading story to all to enjoy.

Michael E. Boblit
D.D.S

Who can resist a time-traveling detective story set in the old west? Not me! The Adventures of Stunning Stephen Edwards as the Stunning Kid in the Time Traveling Marshals took me back to the sixties when I grew up on a steady diet of westerns (Rawhide, Bonanza, Maverick, The Lone Ranger, Wagon Train, etc.). Dodge City in the 1880s has a problem and Davenport, Iowa Detective Rex Tarillo is having a recurring dream in 2016 where the marshal for Dodge City is reaching out for help. Aided by a time machine invented by his brother, Rex and the members of the West Side Kids Detectives agency go back in time to help sort things out, bringing 21st Century knowledge and tools with them. In addition to masked heroes and double-dealing bad guys, there is a healthy helping of "dad jokes" in the book, including some real groaners. The author, who previously wrote motivational books, also included some advice here. One piece of advice in the book seems very appropriate for these days when even people who aren't western heroes are wearing masks, "Courage is being scared to death and saddling up anyway."

Lori Heithoff
Retired Local Government Specialist with
the NYS Department of State.

I loved the time travel theme in David Dorris' new book! It was fun having the characters bring new history into the wild west, and experience the question marks on everyone's faces! Since I recently traveled out west, I could imagine the characters in their setting, which made the book come alive. There were a lot of twists and turns in the storyline, so you didn't know how it was going to end until it ended. Fun to read!!

Robin Rollins
CEO
KOEHLER ELECTRIC

The Adventures of Stunning Stephen Edwards offers something for everyone: adventure, an interesting cast of characters, some fantasy, and a lot of subtle humor. Enjoy!

Joan Tapper
Retired
Mom, Grandma, Great Grandma

I really loved the story. I like how Stephen was helping people out in the old stomping grounds of the west end and Rex remember him helping and needed him to go back in time to help his great great grandfather. Definitely brought back some great memories. It blew my mind how the story made it's twists and turns to the end.

Amy White

The Adventures Of Stunning Stephen Edwards As The Stunning Kid In The Time Traveling Marshals

DAVID DORRIS

authorHOUSE

AuthorHouse™
1663 Liberty Drive
Bloomington, IN 47403
www.authorhouse.com
Phone: 833-262-8899

Published by AuthorHouse 07/30/2020

ISBN: 978-1-7283-6745-3 (sc)
ISBN: 978-1-7283-6746-0 (hc)
ISBN: 978-1-7283-6781-1 (e)

Library of Congress Control Number: 2020913307

Print information available on the last page.

CONTENTS

Acknowledgement

I would like to thank the people behind this book project, Raven Tan, my Check-In-Coordinator, Kristine Rubio, my Publishing Services Associate and the rest of the AuthorHouse team.

Chapter 1

THE DREAM

It is now April 21, 2016 a year after Stunning Stephen Edwards helped two Davenport police Detectives and The West Side Kids Detectives get the evidence that was needed to put Jerry Dickerson and his gang behind bars.

As Davenport Detective Rex Tarillo is waking up this particular morning, he begins to recall a reoccurring dream he has been having for the last week. It seems that his great, great, great grandfather, Rocky Allen has been trying to communicate with Rex in his dreams.

At first Rex thought it was just dreams. In Rex's dream, Rocky Allen would say, "Rex, I need your help. Rex, I need your help. It is April 1880 and I am the town Marshal for Dodge City and I need your help."

This morning it seemed more real than the day before, because this dream was different. In this dream, Rocky Allen added, "I was the Marshal here in Dodge City two years ago. I was really good as a Marshal. There was a bank robbery here in Dodge. One of the gang that robbed the bank was a sixteen year old boy. I shot and killed the boy. I didn't know he was a young boy, because he was masked. I couldn't handle the idea that I killed him and became the town drunk.

In the meantime, The Dean Dickerson gang came to and has taken over the town. The Marshal who took over my job was shot in the back by The Dean Dickerson Gang. One of the gang members name is Ace The Assassin and he lives up to his name. He is a bare handed boxer and fast on the draw.

The Dodge City Mayor is part of the gang. Dean thought I wouldn't be any threat to him and his gang, so he had the Mayor appoint me City Marshal while I was passed out on the floor of Dean Dickerson's Saloon. The Mayor told the crowd in the saloon that he was going to appoint a man with experience. Two men lifted me up to the bar where I sat when the Mayor pinned the star on me.

I asked one of the dance hall girls if I was really the Marshal or was it another trick being played on me. She told me I was really the Marshal.

I then announced to the crowd that I am officially stopping my drinking, because I am choosing the badge over the bottle. Sometimes a man has to stand up and be counted. From now on the law is going to be on the square and respected in this town.

Dean Dickerson offered to be my deputy because the job may be to tough for me. I told him no because I had somebody else in mind who is fast with his gun and fists.

I am now sober, and I need your help. Help me Rex. Help me Rex. Call your brother, Don, and his wife Cat, short for Catherine in Edmond Oklahoma. They have perfected a time machine that can transport you back to 1880."

Chapter 2

THE TIME MACHINE

As Rex was sitting at the table eating breakfast, thoughts began racing through his mind as to what he should do. After Rex was done eating, he called his brother Don and explained to him about his dreams. Next, he asked Don about the time machine he created.

Don explained to Rex that Cat has a business where she is hired to paint the rooms in apartments for landlords. Don is always trying to come up with ideas with his inventions to make money.

A year ago, he started to work on a time machine. He accidentally came across an idea that made his time machine work. Rex then asked Don if he would help him and his associates to go back in time to help their great, great, great grandfather, Rocky Allen.

Don replied, "I have lots of time on my hands. Count me in. Now that my time machine is perfected, I was looking for volunteers to go backward or forward in time."

"As soon as I come up with a plan, I will get back to you," answered Rex.

As the day went on, Rex thought about how he could help his grandfather. Finally, the answer came to him. It was a no brainier. This plan was perfect because Stunning Stephen Edwards was the answer. Stephen is an undefeated professional boxer who is smart, creative, very good with firearms and had two horses. Stephen has also learned the art of being a pick pocket.

Stephen had worked very well with Hannibal and Scooter to put Jerry Dickerson and his crew behind bars. These three men can do the same to Dean Dickerson and his gang. Stephen didn't know it, but he was going to be asked to go back in time as The Stunning Kid.

Rex then picked up his telephone and called The West Side Kids Detective Agency. Scooter answered the phone and started to talk to Rex when he heard Hannibal say to Scooter, "Who are you talking to?"

"It's Detective Rex," answered Scooter. "He wants to come to our office with Detective Columbo at 5:30 p. m. and talk to you, me and my buddy Stephen Edwards."

"Give me that phone!" answered Hannibal. "I'll handle this! Hello Rex. This is Hannibal. What can we possibly do for you at this hour, HMM?"

"I have a huge problem that only you, Scooter and Stephen can handle," explained Rex. "If I can get in touch with Stephen to come to your office at 5:30, I will tell you my problem. You just won't believe what it is. I would like to hire the three of you to help me."

"Of course. Of course. We're here to serve the needy. After trying to catch you as a small fry and working with Stephen and you about making people invisible, I think I will be able to believe anything you told me," answered Hannibal. "It looks like here we go again, and I don't know if I'm going to like that or not."

"That's why I'm asking for your help," pleaded Rex. "You have the special talents to handle these kind of problems. Other people would think I was crazy if I asked them to do what I am going to ask you to do. I will pay the three of you well. Let me get in touch with Stephen and Columbo. We will be at your office at 5:30."

Chapter 3

THE MEETING

It was now 5:30 and Stephen, Hannibal, Scooter, Columbo and Rex began their meeting. Rex began by explaining the dreams he was having followed by calling his brother, Don about his time machine.

"Just how do you think we can help?" asked Stephen.

"I have been thinking about it," replied Rex. "Definitely, I will let you know how this should happen. This will get you started. I have watched Westerns all my life. Even though they are all make believe, I came up with a plan of my own.

Stephen, after working with you as The Invisible Man, I think you can come up with the right kind of schemes, with the help of Scooter and Hannibal to pull it off on Dean Dickerson and his gang.

In this day of age, we are all familiar with heroes that have secret identities."

"Who do you think I should be?" asked Stephen. "Clark Kent and Superman?"

"I want to be Jimmie Olson," requested Scooter. "Hannibal, that means you have to be Perry White."

"No," explained Rex. "I want Stephen to go back in time as an Eastern Dude, Stephen Edwards showing up in a derby hat and a gray suit. You will keep a pearl handled Colt 45 hidden in your boot. You will arrive in Dodge City by stage. Hannibal and Scooter will ride into town on a covered wagon pulled by a team of horses and go to the Marshal's office to be sworn in as Deputies on the QT. I don't want Dean Dickerson to know the three of you know each other and are friends to begin with.

Stephen, I want Dean Dickerson to think you're a pushover who is not a threat to him. After you are made Deputy Marshal, you can then begin to show Dean Dickerson that he better give you respect. You are not going to back down from him because you are going to enforce the law.

Just think of it Stephen. You are an honorary Davenport Police Officer here in April 2016. Your smart enough to be a detective yourself. Now you have the opportunity to go back in time to 1880 in the untamed west to become a Dodge City Deputy Marshal. What do you think of that?"

"It sounds awesome, exciting and I love it," replied Stephen. "1880 sounds fine. I like to study The Civil War and would really like to go back to that time period."

"Not me," laughed Scooter. "The Revolutionary War sounds more interesting to me. Did you know that the battle of Bunker Hill was not on the level? Didn't anybody think that was funny? How about you the reader. Did you laugh because my friends didn't?

If you're not going to laugh at my jokes, then show my how smart you are. Does anybody know if England has a Fourth of July?"

"No," replied Columbo. "England does not have a Fourth of July. Even the reader knows that."

"Everybody has a Fourth of July," explained Scooter. "Nobody goes from the 3rd of July to the 5th.

We all know what happened when the King of England sent his troops to invade America and about Paul Revere, The Midnight Cowboy of 1776. He rode around yelling, "The British are coming." He must have had a nice ride. You may not believe this when I tell you his first stop was at a sleazy motel."

"There weren't any motels back then," corrected Hannibal.

"What are you?" asked Scooter. "A know it all. One of these days, I'm going to read a book and I'll be as smart as you. So, I said motel. What I meant was his first stop was at a sleazy hotel. The point I'm trying to make is that nobody knows how he got his horse up to the 6th floor. There, you satisfied?"

"OK, I get it," replied Hannibal. "Is that supposed to be funny?"

"A lot you know. You just don't have a sense of humor. Now let me continue and try to pay attention what I was saying about Paul Revere when he was making his ride. There was a nut thought to be John Paul Jones. He was from the Jones Family who had their own private war with the Smith Family.

John Paul was seen waving a lantern back and forth, back and forth. He must have been looking for girls, because he believed in life, liberty, and the happiness of pursuit. He was willing to pay their transportation, one by land, two by sea. It must have been fun, or nobody would be doing it."

"Boys let's get back to business and stop this nonsense," ordered Rex. "Stephen, what was your decision about going back in time to 1880?"

"Like I said, I prefer to going back to The Civil War time period," answered Stephen. "If it's necessary to go back to 1880, I will settle for that."

"Does that mean you will do it?" asked Rex.

"You better believe I'll do it," answered Stephen.

"If Stephen is going to do this, I'm going to do this," broke in Scooter.

"I can't believe I'm going to be involved in this nonsense. If Scooter is going to do this with Stephen, then I better go along to keep them both out of trouble," Hannibal informed Rex.

"Stephen's going to have enough to worry about. He won't have time to keep Scooter out of trouble. Stephen, you leave Scooter to me. I guess it's up to me to be the one to keep Scooter out of trouble and see that he is happy."

"That settles that," stated Stephen. "I guess were going to be the Three Musketeers again."

"When we go back in time, is Stephen going to do any bare handed boxing?" asked Scooter. "Somebody told me that Wyatt Earp refereed bare handed boxing matches. If Stephen has a match, can we get Wyatt Earp to be the referee?"

"No Scooter. Our job is to deal with The Dean Dickerson Gang and then to return back home," explained Stephen.

"That's OK," reasoned Scooter. "I would rather meet George Washington anyway. George was a very interesting person. He had dentures made out of wood. It is a well-known fact that his bark was worse than his bite."

"Your making that up about ole George," insisted Hannibal.

"Is that so. Is that so," answered Scooter. "I'm not making this up. Everybody knows about when Washington's Troops wintered in Valley Forge. Are you going to interrupt me again Hannibal?"

"Yes I am. Just what's your point?" asked Hannibal. "Come on genius. Let's hear it."

"I said Washington's Troops wintered in Valley Forge," replied Scooter. "It got down to 10 below zero. It turned out to be The United States first cold war.

Then there was the time that George Washington stood up in a rowboat while he was crossing The Delaware? Do you want to hear about that one?"

"Go ahead and you tell us Scooter. Get it out of your system so we can get on with the meeting," demanded Rex.

"OK, this is the last one about Washington. Just wait until you hear it. You're going to love it," laughed Scooter. "The reason he stood up in the rowboat. Are ready for this one? The reason he stood up in the rowboat was that he was afraid to sit down because somebody would hand him an oar. Doesn't anybody think that is funny, anybody? How about you the reader. Don't you think that's funny?"

"Yes, that was funny," laughed Stephen. "That's enough. If were going back in time, we need to concentrate on what Rex has to tell us, so we don't get into trouble. What else do you have Rex?"

"As I said earlier. Stephen you will have a dual identity. You will appear as The Stunning Kid as needed. Who is The Stunning Kid, you ask? He is just the guy who is going to give Dean Dickerson and his gang something else to worry about. He will tell Dean that Dodge City is now his territory and to stay out of his way, because he works alone.

When you are Stephen Edwards, after you are deputized, you will wear a white Stetson Hat, a yellow neckerchief, a brown checkered shirt and black pants. Your gun belt will have one holster carrying a pearl handled Colt 45. As Stephen Edwards you will ride your white horse Lightning.

When you are The Stunning Kid, you will be wearing A Mexican hat, Mexican shirt and black pants. This gun belt will have two holsters carrying two pearl handled Colt 45's. Then to top it off, you will be wearing a black bandanna over your face. You will take your black horse Thunder back in time to ride as The Stunning Kid.

When you change back and forth from Steven Edwards and The Stunning Kid, all you have to do is change your shirt, hat, gun belts and change from the neckerchief to the bandanna."

"When you talk about Dean, that reminds me of The Dean at The University of Davenport who gave me trouble just because I blew up Rex's new car and broke The Dean's expensive statue twice," added Scooter. "He just couldn't understand that no day is perfect."

"Scooter, after getting to know you, I believe you are a good person. With you, no day is perfect. I don't know what your problem is, but I bet it's hard to pronounce," answered Rex. "But as all of you know, because of everything that happened, I became a 42 inch Small Fry because of what Scooter did. Please don't talk about that anymore. It just gives me nightmares. OK?"

"I'm sorry Rex. I'll try not to talk about it anymore," mumbled Scooter.

"When I go back in time with Hannibal and Rex, who am I going to be? I was counting on being Jimmie Olson."

"No Scooter, you can't go back in time to 1880 and be Jimmie Olson. As I said earlier, you and Hannibal are going be Deputy Marshals working with Marshal Rocky Allen and Stephen?" explained Rex.

"Do I get to be a cowboy and ride a horse?" asked Scooter.

"You sure will," explained Rex. "You and Hannibal will also learn to drive a covered wagon with a team of horses. The team will be Lightning and Thunder. The wagon will be filled with cases of bottled water to put in your canteens. You can also take canned food and other food with you of your choosing along with soap, shaving cream, toilet paper and clothes.

Nobody from that time period, except The Marshal is to know about your supplies. You can have the covered wagon and Thunder hidden at Oliver Columbo's Stables. Oliver is a good friend of Rocky Allen. While the wagon is stored at the stables, Oliver will have horses for you and Hannibal to ride."

"I have a friend who has a horse named Mayo," Scooter went on to say. "Whenever that horse gets upset, then Mayonnaise."

"Stop that Scooter and pay attention to what Rex is saying," ordered Columbo. "I don't know why you can't act like a Sophisticated Private Detective. Someday, I'm going to have to have a long talk with you."

"As I was saying," Rex continued to say, "Stephen will teach Hannibal and you in a week about firearms, riding a horse and all the things you need to know. While you're at it, you can come up with plans of your own as to confronting The Dean Dickerson Gang. When you're this close to danger, you have to be ready for anything."

"Can we take the chemicals with us to make us invisible?" asked Hannibal.

"No, I think you need to come up with a different strategy," noted Rex. "I'm sure the three of you can come up with a different plan to confuse Dean Dickerson and get the evidence to put him and his gang behind bars.

All right today is the 21st of April. You have one week to prepare for this new adventure. I need the sizes of clothes and shoes you wear. I know a place here in The Quad Cities where I can get you the clothes you need for that time period. My brother Don and I will meet you on the farm where Stephen is boarding his horses on April 28 at 6 p. m."

Chapter 4

GOING TO DODGE CITY 1880

It is now April 28, 6 p. m. Rex has spent the week getting in touch with Rocky Allen through his dreams about his plans to send Stephen, Hannibal, and Scooter back to 1880. Rex also has all the supplies with him for Stephen, Hannibal, and Scooter. Columbo, Rex's brother Don and his time machine is also with him. As the stage is set to send these heroes back in time, Don realizes he forgot to tell Rex something about his time machine.

"Rex, I just remembered something about my time machine," informed Don. "I can send these boys into the past without any trouble. It just dawned on me. I'm not sure I can bring them back home. They could be stuck back in 1880 in Dodge City."

"I'm sorry boys," ordered Rex. "The assignment is off, finished. I don't want to risk losing the three of you to the past. We just can't help Marshal Rocky Allen."

"I don't know about Hannibal and Scooter, but I still want to do this," explained Stephen. "You and Don can work on my return after I'm gone. We all have our special talents. I believe in you Rex. If your brother Don is smart enough to send us back in time, he can figure out as to how to bring us back to the present."

"If Stephen wants to go back in time, then I want to go," mumbled Scooter. "The Lone Ranger doesn't go anywhere without Tonto. I know I am always doing something stupid. Even so, he will need somebody he can depend on. I will be Tonto, and I will try to help him the best I can."

"What about you, Hannibal?" asked Rex. "You don't have to go because these two want to go."

"No, no and no, I don't want to go," blurted out Hannibal. "These are my friends and I can't back out of going. If I let them go without me, I will have tremendous nightmares. I know they are going to need me to get them out of the troubles they are going to encounter with The Dean Dickerson Gang. I guess I'm going, so Head Em Up and Move Em Out."

"Alright boys. If you really want to do this, I'm going to give each of you something that looks like a quarter," explained Don. "Keep this on you at all times. This is still not practical to send you anywhere in time until I do more research on the time machine. Don't make things worse and loose that coin I gave you. This is how I'm going to be able to keep track of where you're at and what you're doing.

Rex, after I hit this button on the time machine, I will need you to help me to keep track of the boys. I have work to do to make sure I can get these boys home. I have to get this taken care of in short order."

"One last question," reasoned Hannibal. "When you are sure. When you're really sure. When you're absolutely positive you can bring us home, would you be able to send the rest of The West Side Kids to Dodge City in case we need help?" asked Hannibal.

"Just to make sure we can get you all back," answered Don. "I want to bring one of you back to the present to make sure I have this figured out on how to bring you all back.

With that coin I gave you, we can talk back and forth through the time machine. When you need extra help, we can send it. When I want to bring one of you back, we can talk it over about when it would be a good time to try it. When I'm sure it works, I can bring you back if you get into trouble."

In an instant, Don hit the button on his time machine and The Three Musketeers was heading for Dodge City, Kansas, 1880. Moments later, they appeared on a hill overlooking a dirt road, three miles outside Dodge City. Stephen was wearing a suit with a derby hat from that era. Thunder and Lightning still had their saddles on. It was time to hitch them to the wagon.

As Stephen, Hannibal and Scooter stood next to their covered wagon full of supplies, they looked down on the dirt road. A woman dressed in black was riding a runaway horse.

"It's a runaway," yelled Stephen as he jumped on the back of Lightning and rode after the woman as a clumsy horseback rider, trying to keep from falling off Lightning.

As Stephen approached the woman and her horse, he reached out and grabbed the bridle to the woman's horse, stopping, it, and falling off of Lightning on to the ground.

Stephen then walked over to the woman and helped her out of the saddle as she fainted in his arms. Seconds later the woman began to open her eyes as she was still in Stephen's arms.

"Dixie, Dixie Doneright, what happened to spook your horse?" asked Stephen.

"A rattle snake scared my horse and I lost control," answered the woman. "My name is not Dixie Doneright. It's Belle Doneright. You have a sincere face and are a handsome dude from the east. Now that I think of it, I like the rest of you. You just risked your life to save my life."

"I'm Stephen Edwards," replied Stephen. "Big horses scare me, and I don't ride very good. Those boys up on the hill gave me this horse to try and save you. I have to return the horse to them. Does the stage come down this road?"

"You're in luck. The stage should be coming down this road in about thirty minutes," explained Belle. "I owe you for saving my life. I would take you back to Dodge on my horse, but I am late for an appointment. I would have gotten there sooner if you hadn't rescued me. I have a saloon in Dodge called Belle's Saloon. You stop in there anytime and I will buy you a drink.

I should be running into the stage on my way down the road. I will tell the driver to be watching for you. I have to go now. Don't forget to stop in at my saloon to see me."

As Belle rode away, Stephen rode back up the hill where Hannibal and Scooter was waiting.

"What was that all about?" asked Hannibal.

"Rescuing that woman on her runaway horse was luck," said Stephen informing Hannibal and Scooter. "You won't believe this. I couldn't believe it. I could have sworn that it was Dixie Doneright. She looks just like Dixie, only her name is Belle Doneright and she owns a saloon in Dodge."

"Could she be related to Dixie Doneright, Jerry Dickerson's girl?" asked Scooter.

"There are a lot of coincidences between Jerry Dickerson and his gang and Dean Dickerson and his gang," admitted Stephen. "I don't know what's going on here. We just have to go into Dodge and find out.

Let's get Thunder and Lightning hitched up to the wagon and then you two go into Dodge. Find the Marshal and then get sworn in as Deputies. Then tell the Marshal that you want to have his friend Oliver Columbo hide Thunder and store the covered wagon at his stable. Have him put Lightning in a stall until I need him. Tell the Marshal that I will be coming into Dodge on the stage. Remember, when I get there, you don't know me."

"Scooter are you paying attention to what Stephen just said?" asked Hannibal. "Don't do something stupid when you see Stephen. When we see Stephen, we have to pretend we don't know him to fool Dean Dickerson and his gang."

"I don't like pretending that I don't know Stephen because he is my friend," replied Scooter. "Hannibal, because you and Stephen are both my friends, I will do as you say."

Within minutes, Hannibal and Scooter was on their way to Dodge while Stephen walked back down the hill to the dirt road waiting for the stage. Thirty minutes later the stage was in sight, coming down the dirt road. Stephen began waving his arms for the stage to stop. Stephen was told to get in by the driver. As Stephen sat down in the coach next to a big man, a young lady was sitting across from him.

"I'm Stephen Edwards. What are your names?" inquired Stephen.

"Your last name is Edwards," replied the young lady. "What a coincidence. My name is Marilyn, Marilyn Edwards."

"It is a coincidence. I have a great, great, great grandmother by the name of Marilyn Edwards." Turning to the big man, Stephen asked, "Who are you?"

"Most people know me as Smitty, The Grim Reaper," answered the man. "My friends just call me Smitty."

As Stephen continued to talk to Smitty and Marilyn, the stage entered Dodge City and came to a stop.

Chapter 5
THE NEW DEPUTY MARSHAL IS HERE

There in front of the depot stood The Marshal with Deputy Marshal Hannibal and Deputy Marshal Scooter waiting for Stephen to climb out of the coach.

"Finally, Stephen Edwards is here and ready to clean up Dodge through law and order. If you insist on breaking the law, Stephen will pull your leg off and spank you with it," exclaimed Marshal Allen as Smitty climbed out of the coach. "Stephen, you old horse thief. Your finally here to be my Deputy."

"I'm not Stephen," answered the big man. "My name is Smitty, The Grim Reaper. I'm the trail boss of a herd of cattle that is twenty miles south of Dodge."

Stephen then climbed out of the coach holding a parasol in his right hand and a bird cage in his left hand, followed by Marilyn.

"If you're looking for Stephen Edwards, you found him. That's me," Stephen informed The Marshal.

The crowd immediately burst into laughter.

"Oh, oh, what have we got here?" asked Lefty. "So, your Stephen Edwards. I've heard of you. I tried to figure out what you looked like. Seeing you climb out of the coach with a parasol and a birdcage in your hands is worth a thousand words.

I see that The Marshall already has two new Deputies. So, your Deputy number three, The Deputy that's going to clean up Dodge. It's just our luck, because you look like the toughest of the bunch. How are you going to clean up Dodge? Are you going to use brains against brawn, your superior intelligence?"

Again, the crowd burst into laughter.

"That is my intent," answered Stephen. "We all know why I'm here. I'm not here to win a popularity contest. It may sound impossible. I'm not going to put up with outlaws in these parts.

Our country is great, and we should honor our flag. Settlers from other all over the world have come to Dodge and the surrounding territories for a better life, because we have been blessed with liberty. As everybody knows, we are all fortunate to have equal opportunity and should be equally obligated.

Our country is not perfect and that includes Dodge City. I'm going to do everything I can for the security of Dodge City, because it comes first. I'm here to make a change for the better. I believe dignity should be given to all and when I become a Deputy Marshal, I'm going to protect everybody's rights and privileges.

Dodge started out as a village and now it's a town. Someday it's going to be a metropolis. The law is going to rule and I'm here to take things in my own hands to get the job done."

"Stephen, get rid of that parasol and bird cage so you can come to the office and get sworn in," instructed Marshal Allen. "I never thought I would see my Deputy as a laughing stock.

I told everybody that the only thing that can stop a badman with a gun is a good man with a gun. When you come to Dodge, they was going to see a real tough gunfighter and love it. If anybody breaks the law, you will pull their leg off and spank them with it. I'm afraid you're giving everybody the wrong idea about you. Any more of this and I'm going out of my mind."

"That can wait," answered Stephen. "First I want to help Marilyn find a room and get settled."

A woman from the crowd walked up to Marilyn and told her she can stay at her boarding house.

"Now that that is taken care of," said Ace, "We want to take our new Deputy Marshal into Belle's Saloon and buy him a drink."

"Forget that Stephen. Let's go to my office now, to get sworn in!" ordered The Marshal.

"I don't really see the need to rush," answered Stephen. "I get the feeling that I caused some inconvenience to everybody. I'm sure that Ace and Lefty want to check me out. Because I don't like the smell of things, I want to know more about Ace and Lefty. After all, if I'm going to be part of Dodge City, I want to get to know everybody and I will start by letting Ace buy me a drink and then I will be over directly. Let's go Ace, get your money out."

Stephen, Ace, Lefty, Hannibal, and Scooter then walked into Belle's Saloon with the crowd following. As Stephen walked into the saloon he said, "This saloon doesn't look like much. I'm sure after your here awhile, you will get to hate it."

The crowd began to laugh as Stephen walked up to the bar. Ace asked, "What are you going to have big man?"

"A nice sarsaparilla," answered Stephen.

"I want to buy you a man's drink," insisted Ace as he stood behind Stephen.

"And just what is wrong with sarsaparilla?" asked Stephen. "Sarsaparilla is just another name for root beer. Someday there will be a restaurant chain that specializes in selling root beer."

"Bartender bring over a big tall glass of whiskey for our fearless Deputy Marshal," instructed Ace. "If he's going to be the tough, fearless Deputy Marshal that upholds law and order, he needs to be drinking a man's drink instead of this root beer."

"I'm not a Deputy Marshal," explained Stephen. "I haven't been sworn in yet."

After the whiskey was set in front of Stephen, Ace pulled his gun and stuck it in Stephen's back.

"Now drink it all down like a good Deputy Marshal," insisted Ace.

"I told you Ace, I'm not a Deputy Marshal," Stephen repeated.

"It looks like you're afraid to drink the whiskey and you're afraid of me," roared Ace. "Don't get encouraged to try something stupid. I have a loaded gun in your back. If you don't drink the whiskey, you're not going to live to be a Deputy Marshal."

"What a clever idea. It looks like there is no simple way to get around this. OK, I give up. You win. I will take your advice," replied Stephen. "Ace, I wouldn't call me afraid too often and one more time is too often. I have a question for you. Do you like your front teeth, true or false?"

Before Ace could answer Stephen picked up the glass of whiskey and threw the whiskey over his right shoulder into Ace's face. Stephen immediately turned around and hit Ace in his face with a right hand, knocking Ace on the floor. With the gun still in Ace's hand, Stephen kicked the gun out of his hand, across the floor.

Just then Belle came out of her second floor office and walked halfway down the stairs as Dean Dickerson walked up to Stephen and asked him what was going on.

"Look at Belle," exclaimed Rhonda, one of the dance hall girls. "She just got back from her ride. The way she is looking at Stephen, she knows something is going on here with Stephen. She don't know whether to kiss him or shoot him."

"It seems that Ace and I just had a little disagreement as to what I should be drinking," explained Stephen as he brushed against Dean. "We can't win them all, but we can try."

"Ace how did this Deputy Marshal knock you on the floor?" inquired Dean. "You're supposed to be a Bare Handed Boxing Champion."

"He hit me with his right hand," explained Ace. "It had to be a sneaky punch. I never expected him to lead with his right."

Stephen then walked over to Ace, reaching out with his right hand, and helped Ace stand up.

"Well, Mister Deputy Marshal," ordered Dean. "I have a hobby collecting Deputy Marshal's guns. Give me your gun or am I going to have trouble with you?"

"As I told Ace, I am now going to tell you the same thing. I'm not a Deputy Marshal yet and I don't carry a gun. Am I going to have trouble with you?" answered Stephen as he held up his suit coat to show he didn't have one.

"People are always surprised that I don't carry one. I was told before I accepted the position of being a Deputy Marshal that you were very tough to deal with. I have to hand it to you. I can't fight your logic. I was told that you have to get up pretty early in the morning to fool Dean Dickerson.

What you have in your veins is ice water. Even when your happy, your nasty and because of that you can be very inhuman. You may be greedy, but not crazy. It's lucky that I didn't have a gun. One of us might have gotten hurt and if it was me, I wouldn't like it, would I?"

"That is very lucky for you," answered Dean as everybody began to laugh.

"What can you tell me about Edwards?" asked Dean.

"Who, Marilyn Edwards? She is a nice looking young woman that I rode in with on the stage," answered Stephen.

"The Edwards I'm talking about has a mustache," corrected Dean.

"It looks like we're talking about two different girls," explained Stephen as everybody began to laugh again.

"The Edwards I'm talking about is you with the mustache," explained Dean. "I want straight answers to my questions. We all know your Stephen Edwards. Just who is Stephen Edwards?"

"I'm glad you asked me that question. I've had a long time to get used to it. I always believe I'm a failure at everything I try to do," answered Stephen. "I'm glad I caught you in a good mood to discuss this with you."

"What makes you think you're a failure or that I'm even in a good mood?" questioned Dean. "Did you discuss this with the Marshal before you took the job as a Deputy Marshal? Why don't you tell him the truth?"

"I can't. It's too painful. You sure don't have a good memory. I'm the guy who is going to be Dodge City's new Deputy Marshal that is supposed to be cleaning up Dodge City. Just when I try to get something done like the job I'm supposed to do here in Dodge, something goes wrong. I would rather be a live failure than a dead hero," explained Stephen as Rhonda walked up to Stephen with a bucket full of water and a mop.

"Take this mop and bucket," offered Rhonda. "Now you can start to clean up Dodge."

Again, everybody laughed as Stephen picked up the mop and put the end with the cloth in the bucket. He then put the mop over his right shoulder with the wet cloth of the mop behind him. Next, he turned to the right with the cloth end of the wet mop hitting Rhonda in the face.

"You clumsy oaf", yelled Rhonda.

"I'll get you for that. This is a private fight and I owe you for that Sunday punch you gave me. Now you're going to have to fight me next and I'm going to pin your ears back," said Ace as he walked toward Stephen.

Just as Ace put up his hands to fight, Stephen set down the mop and gave Ace a jab, followed by a right cross, finished with a left hook overhand right combination and Ace was again knocked to the floor. Stephen then picked up the bucket of water and dumped the water all over Ace.

"That wasn't so tough. Ace it looks like you just won't learn," exclaimed Stephen.

"There he is. The Fearless Bare Handed Boxing Champion knocked on the floor again," shouted Dean. "You beat Biceps Bill and The Bone Crusher in two separate bare handed boxing matches, one round to the finish. How can you let this Deputy Marshall do this to you? You want everybody to think this is the best you can do? You bring shame on yourself."

"The way he fights is different than what I have ever seen, and he is killing me," said a puzzled Ace.

"Oh fine. Just fine. What is the matter with you?" question Dean. "It seems you have been doing everything but the right way. You have been doing the same thing over and over again expecting different results. What do you think you are, on a picnic? Somebody give you the day off?

It looks like you are not on the alert as to how he is fighting, and you are taking unnecessary chances. Timing is very important. You need to have a diversion, move fast and be on the alert as to how Stephen is fighting. Your letting this Deputy Marshal get the best of you. You're not living up to your name, Ace, The Assassin."

"Ace don't take it so hard. We all know that you're a flake. You have guts but no brains. If dynamite was brains, you wouldn't have enough to blow your nose," laughed Stephen. "So far we have a champ on the floor. It is hard to live up to a name like that when you're always laying on the floor.

What a beautiful shiner you have in your right eye from when I hit you before. Now you're going to have a shiner in your left eye to match. It looks like you not going to be much good for a while."

"This isn't over," replied Ace. "You can't be lucky all the time. Next time I'm going to take it out of your hide."

"This better be over. All you want to do is cause trouble by fanning the fire. You think you're so good that you can scare me to death. Don't you know you can't beat me?

I never look for a fight, but if I have to fight you again, I'm going to clean your clock. I don't have to make sure that I win because you're not even a challenge." explained Stephen. "You better back down and forget your thoughts of revenge and consider the repercussions.

It seems to me that your lights are on and there is nobody home. If you show me disrespect by trying to sink your fist in my jaw again, next time I'm going to pummel your face to make you look uglier than you are and then I'm going to put your lights out.

I'm a professional boxer and I train hard to keep my body in shape. I never wrestle with an animal, especially a pig. You both get dirty and some animals such as a pig likes it. That must be why you like laying on the floor.

Dean, just as you collect Deputy Marshal's guns, I collect bullets. Would you mind if I borrow a couple of guns for a minute?"

"Go ahead. Be my guest. Just don't shoot yourself," replied Dean.

"I want guns from Ace, Lefty, The Mayor, Belle and you," requested Stephen. "If you don't mind, I will be shooting at those small eight round decorations on the wall across the room."

"Go ahead," offered Dean. "I'm not worrying about you hitting them from here unless you're going to be one of those sharpshooters."

Stephen then picked up Dean's gun hitting one of the decorations in the center, followed by the guns of Lefty, The Mayor and Belle all hitting the decorations dead center. With four decorations left, Stephen picked up Ace's gun, fanning it, hitting the last four decorations dead center as everybody's mouth flew open in surprise.

As Dean was turning to give Stephen a surprised look, he noticed a watch chain hanging out of Ace's shirt pocket.

"Ace, what are you doing with a watch chain hanging out of your shirt pocket?" asked Dean. "You never carry a pocket watch."

Ace looked down at his shirt pocket in surprise and pulled it out of his pocket with a gold watch hanging on the end of the chain.

"That's not my watch," quoted a surprised Ace. "I wonder how that got there?"

"You should know," insisted Dean. "You're the one person I thought I could trust. That's my watch. You took it from me and put it in your pocket. The chain fell out of your pocket after Stephen hit you and you fell to the floor. It looks like I can't trust you anymore."

"You can trust me, Boss," answered Ace. "I really can't explain how it ended up in my pocket."

"You can't explain it because you put it there," replied Dean. "What else have you taken of mine? Oh right, oh, right. Let's hear it."

"Nothing Boss. I haven't taken anything of yours," insisted Ace. "We have a good thing going here, you and me. What can I do to prove it to you?"

"Are you quite finished. That is the most innocent thing for you to say. You have no proof, none. You need me. Sometimes I wonder if I need you. If I paid you what you're worth, that would add up to nothing. Let's go to my office," ordered Dean. "I have a job for you. There better not be any slip ups. I'm going to keep my eye on you and see how you do."

Just then Stephen grabbed Dean's arm and said to him, "You look tired, very tired. Are you feeling OK? You better sit down in this chair and relax for a minute."

"I have been feeling tired. How can I relax when I have to put up with the likes of Ace? This is how the battle goes with Ace. Sometimes he makes me so mad that I want to split his lip," sighed Dean. "I have a lot of responsibilities with this saloon and the people who work for me. Do you know what the real nightmare is? You have to have a stubborn streak to run this outfit when the men give you trouble. Even though I'm the boss, sometime the men try telling me what to do."

"I have a solution. I'm surprised you didn't think of it. Now is your big chance. What you need to do is put Lefty in charge although he will be taking orders from you. Then you need to go down to the creek north of town and camp, fish, and rest until you feel better," suggested Stephen.

"I think that's a dandy idea," replied Dean. "I really do feel very tired."

"What is The Deputy blabbing about?" asked Ace.

"Ace, I think it's necessary for both you and Lefty to come to my office to have a chat, now," ordered Dean. "Ace, I changed my mind. The job I had for you concerning The Wilson Homestead, I'm going to give to Lefty."

"Dean, when your done talking to Ace and Lefty," ordered Belle who was still standing halfway down the stairs, "I want you to come to my office."

Stephen then walked over to the wall with his pocketknife out saying, "I told you I collect bullets."

He then pulled the bullets out of the wall with his knife and left for The Marshal's Office with Hannibal and Scooter while Ace and Lefty followed Dean to his office.

"I think that new Deputy Marshal is going to be a problem," said Dean to Ace and Lefty. "Lefty, take Danny, Shorty and Mugs and stampede the cattle in the holding pens through the town past The Marshal's Office and shoot up the town. When this new Deputy Marshal comes out to stop you, maybe he might get hit with a stray bullet. After that, I want you to head for The Wilson Homestead and chase those Nesters off that property."

"You got it Boss," promised Lefty. "I have to go to the stable and get my pinto. It's on the way to the holding pens."

Chapter 6

It's A Trap

As Stephen entered The Marshal's Office, Rocky Allen shouted to Stephen, "Where have you been so long? Why was it so important for you to go into Belle's Saloon instead of coming to my office to get sworn in as my Deputy Marshal?"

"I'm sorry Marshal," replied Stephen. "Don't forget, it was you asking Rex to help you. Rex came to Hannibal, Scooter and me and asked us to help you and he sent us back in time. Before we were sent here, Rex and the three of us had a plan to clean up Dodge City. We was also told that there is a chance we may not be able to get back home.

Rex didn't want Dean to think I was a threat to him right away. That's why I came to town on the stage and got off the coach the way I did. When I saw a chance to see who I was up against, I took it."

"I'm sorry Stephen. I didn't know," reasoned The Marshal. "When everybody laughed at you as you got off the stage, I was disappointed in who you seem to be and I wanted to get you over to my office right away."

After The Marshal swore Stephen in as a Deputy Marshal he replied, "We need a good lawman around here."

"I have some bullets that I want you to keep for me," explained Stephen to The Marshal. "I want to have each bullet labeled as to whose gun they came out of. This information could be very useful later on."

"How can that make a difference?" asked The Marshal.

"If we could dig up the body of The Marshal who was shot in the back, one of these bullets may match," explained Stephen as he heard shooting and cattle out in the street.

Stephen then looked out the window as the cattle was running down the street, causing destruction to the boardwalks as people were running to safety. There was Lefty riding his pinto with Danny, Shorty and Mugs shooting up the town.

"Marshal don't go out there. I'm pretty sure it's a trap," ordered Stephen. "You boys stay here and keep under cover. I'm going out there and do a little scouting around."

"Come on boys, we need to help Stephen. It looks like you're going to need some help," insisted The Marshal.

"It's better that you stay out of sight," instructed Stephen.

"It's no fair being a Deputy when Stephen is having all the fun," cried Scooter. "Oh, dog gone. I always lose out on everything. That's the story of my life."

"You best do as I say Scooter. Your voice could stampede a herd," laughed Stephen. "I will be back in a few minutes. I want to see who is doing all the shooting."

A couple minutes later Stephen heard Lefty yell, "The Deputy Marshal must be asleep, or he is hiding. This puts a different light on things. Let's head to The Wilson Homestead. With The Deputy Marshal out of the way, it will be easy pickings."

Stephen quickly went back to The Marshal's Office and warned The Marshal that the gang left town to go to The Wilson Homestead.

"Who owns a pinto horse?" asked Stephen.

"It's one of Dean Dickerson's men, Lefty," answered The Marshal.

"He must be one of the guys we're after," suggested Stephen. "Now that we're all here, would you tell us just what kind of laws The Dean Dickerson Gang are breaking? What are they in to?"

"They are swindling Homesteaders and chasing them off their land to get in control of the water rights of the lake and creeks," explained Marshal Allen. "They rob and kill at will. They are robbing stages, banks, printing counterfeit $20, $50 and $100 bills and even murder."

Stephen, Hannibal, and Scooter explained their plans to clean up Dodge. They also told The Marshal that everybody must think that Stephen never met Hannibal and Scooter before. Hannibal will now be known as Colorado and Scooter will be called Buster.

Then Stephen went on to tell The Marshal about how he is going to be The Masked Stunning Kid. The plan was to have wanted posters of The Stunning Kid made up and put up around town to give Dean Dickerson and his gang something else to think about.

As Stephen was finished talking, a fifteen year old boy came through the door yelling, "Marshal, Marshal. There are masked men out at my parent's homestead forcing them to pack up our belongings, put them in our wagon and move off our land."

Chapter 7

THE STUNNING KID ENTERS

"Who are your parents and where is your homestead?" Stephen asked.

"Chester and Nora Wilson are my parents. And their homestead is three miles out the road north of Dodge by the creek," answered the boy.

"You wait outside," instructed Stephen. "The Marshal will be with you in a minute."

"Marshal, where is the livery stable?" asked Stephen. "I need to go to the stable to get a change of clothes and Thunder. It's time for The Stunning Kid to appear for the first time as a mysterious masked rider, who is a champion of justice and on the side of the law. I think it's time for The Stunning Kid to try his luck where others have failed."

"Mysterious masked rider. Champion of justice. What movie did you get that out of?" asked Hannibal.

"Do you mind? Do you mind? I didn't get it out of any movie. I don't know why. I just felt like saying it. I guess I'm just trying to get my mind on what I have to do next," answered Stephen. "Hannibal, twenty five minutes after I leave, that's after the big hand on your watch moves twenty five spaces, come with The Marshal and Scooter to the homestead."

As Stephen was going out the door The Marshal demanded, "Boys, keep your mind on what we're doing here."

Twenty minutes later, The Stunning Kid was approaching the Wilson's house where he saw Mr. and Mrs. Wilson loading their belongings into a wagon. Standing by the wagon with guns drawn was four masked men.

The Stunning Kid rode Thunder up to some tall bushes and climbed down from Thunder. He then made his way undetected up to the house, stopping twenty feet from the wagon hiding behind a tree.

"Hurry up and get that wagon loaded," instructed one of the masked men. "After you get it loaded, get off this land and stay off."

"This is our home and our land. My son has gone for The Marshal. When he gets here, you won't be able to make us leave," said Mr. Wilson as The Stunning Kid approached the loaded wagon with both guns drawn.

"OK boys drop your guns and pull down those masks. Who are you working for?" ordered The Stunning Kid.

One of the masked men turned to fire his gun at The Stunning Kid, only The Stunning Kid was faster and shot the gun out of his hand.

"That was just a warning shot. Anybody else want to play? Next time I'll shoot first before you bushwhackers can take a shot at me and then I will ask questions later," explained The Stunning Kid. "Now drop those guns or the next person won't be so lucky. Get those masks down and now."

As the masks were pulled down, Mr. Wilson announced to The Stunning Kid, "These men are Dean Dickerson's men, Lefty, Danny, Shorty and Mugs."

"Dean Dickerson isn't going to like this," warned Lefty. "What's going on here? Who are you and what do you want?"

"I didn't think you looked smart enough to be the boss of this gang. I thought there was somebody bigger than you around here. Tell your boss I'm all chocked up. You can't make an omelet without breaking a few eggs," replied The Stunning Kid.

"I am known as The Stunning Kid. This is my territory now and I work alone. A thief cannot trust another thief, so I don't want to work with anyone."

"This could be serious because Dean Dickerson is not going to give up this territory to you or anybody. It can mean trouble," replied Lefty. "It would be better if we could make a deal with you. I don't suppose you want to talk about it."

"I don't make deals," answered The Stunning Kid. "Is that the best you can think of to scare me? You tell this Dean Dickerson if he starts trouble with me, I will let him hear what trouble sounds like, because I like to fight.

He has to decide not to waste his time and my time or I'll have to have a word with old blood and guts. Dean Dickerson's time is my time, so tell him to stay out of this territory, because now it's mine."

"Why the mask?" asked Lefty. "Are you a Mexican bandit?"

"It doesn't make any difference who I am. As far as your concerned I'm your worst nightmare. To answer your question about my mask, I'm in hiding and every time you see it, it's going to give you more trouble than you think is possible," answered The Stunning Kid.

"Get that hombre, Lefty. You're not going to let This Stunning Kid get away with that are you?" asked Danny. "Tell us what to do."

The Stunning Kid then aimed the forty five he had in his right hand and shot at the ground in front of Lefty three times.

"I'm backing The Marshal and his new Deputies to the best of my ability," promised The Stunning Kid. "I'm the one who is giving the orders. Lefty, your going back to town with me. I'm turning you over to The Marshal so he can take you to jail and you can tell him your story. It's time for the rest of you to leave! Turn your tails and git! Get out of here and don't come back!"

Danny, Shorty, and Mugs then ran to their horses as Danny said, "I would rather be a live coward than a dead hero." The gang mounted their horses and rode off as fast as they could without looking back.

"Well Mr. Stunning Kid, just who are you? I suppose you want me and my family to get off of our homestead just like those other varmints?" asked Mr. Wilson.

"No Mr. Wilson. I'm afraid you've got me wrong. I'm glad you're alright. Now you can start to breathe. Pull yourself together.

I believe that our purpose in life is to help others. I'm a friend and I'm here to help. If I can't help you, I don't want to hurt you. Nobody

30

is going to make you get off of your homestead. This should be free soil to land hungry settlers like you," replied The Stunning Kid.

"In fact, I saw The Marshal and two of his Deputies coming this way. I can't stay. I want you to take charge of the prisoner. Turn him over to The Marshal. When he gets here, he will take Lefty back to Dodge and put him in the calaboose. Lefty, The Marshal and his Deputies will help you unload your wagon."

"You have done me a great favor. How can I ever repay you for what you have done?" asked Mr. Wilson. "Who can I turn to for help if these boys come back?"

"You don't owe me anything. You homesteaders need to band together. If were going to break up that gang, we can't overlook anything. They must be stopped at once. When it comes time for a showdown with Mr. Dean Dickerson, I may need your help to round up the whole gang," explained The Stunning Kid.

"It's about time we have somebody around here that doesn't run like a frightened rabbit when that gang shows up. I admire your courage," replied Mr. Wilson. "Me and the other homesteaders are in a lot of trouble with this gang. I'm calling a meeting of the homesteaders. I'm fed up with this whole thing. We're going to have to fight fire with fire. It looks like we're going to have to hire gunmen like The Dean Dickerson Gang.

This isn't the kind of country a man comes for his health. If we don't do something soon, we'll have to give this territory back to the outlaws."

"That's the worst thing you can do is give up," answered The Stunning Kid. "Just remember, this is your land, your home. You and the other homesteaders need to get out there and fight. Courage is being afraid to saddle up and fight, but you do it anyway."

"You've got a lot of fire in you and your kind of sharp. We really need your help," pleaded Mr. Wilson. "Can we hire you to help us?"

"I'm sorry but I don't hire my guns to anybody," answered The Stunning Kid. "As I said, I work alone. When I decide it's time for me to leave, I don't want to be stopped from going."

"Then I'll tell you what you can do," suggested Mr. Wilson. "There is supposed to be a new Deputy Marshal in Dodge that is supposed to be tough as nails. His name is Stephen Edwards. If you two can work together, the two of you may get the job done."

"That's a great idea. I don't think that Deputy Marshal will work with the likes of me. I know more about him than you think I do. If you have any more ideas like that, let me know," answered The Stunning Kid. "If I give you my word that I will keep Dean Dickerson and his gang busy, will you do what I say about going ahead with your idea of getting all the homesteaders working together? The way I have it planned, we can't lose. The Marshal is coming. I better leave now."

Chapter 8

THE CRAZIEST THING HAPPENED

Twenty minutes later, Danny, Mugs and Shorty was in Dean Dickerson's office telling of their run in with The Stunning Kid.

"Why are you back so soon? Where is Lefty?" asked Dean. "You did get The Wilson's to move off their homestead?"

"You know, the craziest thing happened when we were at The Wilson Homestead," replied Danny. "A masked hombre showed up and chased us away from the homestead. He had two blazing guns and murder in his heart. I asked him who he was. He told us that he was a wanted outlaw by the name of The Stunning Kid.

He said to tell you that he is backing The Marshal and this territory is his now. The Marshal was on his way to The Wilson's Homestead. He cocked those pistols and told Lefty to stay with him and for us to move on and don't look back. He also told us to tell you to leave for other parts because he is going to be tough to deal with."

"I just knew I should have sent Ace with you to get the job done but the new Deputy, Stephen Edwards talked me out of it. Now were going to have to do something about this Stunning Kid. The next time he gets in your way, find out who he is and bring him to me," instructed Dean. "I want all that land by the creek and lake to get all the water rights. We can make a fortune selling the water to the cattlemen. We can buy the land cheap or get it for nothing when these ranchers and homesteaders move away. I could also use those cabins for a price, to hide those hombres two shakes ahead of the law."

"We need to get Lefty out of jail. The Marshal can't hold him because he is The Town Marshal. Mr. Wilson's Homestead is out of his jurisdiction," reasoned Danny. "The next time we go on a raid to get more land, we need to have Ace go with us. If The Stunning Kid shows up, we need to set a trap for him."

Chapter 9

THE MAGIC LANTERN

It was now getting time to fix dinner. Hannibal who is now Deputy Marshal Colorado and Scooter, Deputy Marshal Buster head down to the stables to get supplies out of their covered wagon.

"Rex supplied us with the instant coffee, but he didn't get us any sugar," Buster informed Colorado.

"I guess we need to take what supplies we have to The Marshal's Office and then go over to the General Store to buy some sugar," Colorado replied.

"Colorado, I've been thinking," proposed Buster.

"Does that hurt?" Colorado asked.

"Will you listen to me for a minute?" growled Colorado. "I don't like my name Colorado. Do you like Buster for your name?"

"No, I don't," answered Buster. "These names just don't sound right for us. Let's just use our own names. I agree. Our own names it is," replied Scooter.

"Do you want to know something Scooter?" asked Hannibal.

"I sure do," replied Scooter.

"Maybe someday you will," laughed Hannibal. "I always said that your IQ wouldn't make a respectable earthquake."

"Very funny. Just who do you think you are, Einstein?" laughed Scooter. "Some Detective you are. One of these days, somebody is going to convince you that two plus two is not five."

Ten minutes later, Colorado who is now Hannibal and Buster who is now Scooter are standing at the counter in the General Store ordering sugar. As our two heroes begin to leave, Scooter stops to pick up a colorful lantern.

"Put that lantern down unless you plan to buy it! That's an expensive lantern!" yelled an anxious store owner just as Belle and Ace was coming through the door. "Who is this man? What are you doing here?"

The lantern then slipped out of Scooter's hands, falling on the floor in pieces.

"Gulp, Hannibal, I did something stupid. What else!" yelled Scooter. "Some no account must have greased that lantern!"

"Would you mind telling me what you're doing? What in the tar nation is the matter with you? I don't want to criticize, but what were you holding the lantern for anyway?" questioned an angry Hannibal. "Who do you think you are, John Paul Jones and you are looking for girls?"

"Hold your horses! You're having a stampede that will cost you $50.00 for breaking that lantern!" shouted the store owner.

"Do you mind? Do you mind? That's a very deleterious accusation and a very fallacious statement. Let's not lose our temper. You sound like you've got distemper and you need a distemper shot," explained Hannibal. "I don't like to sound perpendicular. Yes, Scooter dropped the lantern and broke it and it turned out to be an architectural destruction. He was defused and didn't do this for laughs. He didn't have a crystal ball to tell him that you was going to yell at him and make him drop the lantern.

I want to enumerate that you have a degenerated opinion and what you said was enlightening. I don't want you to jump to seclusion's and get a severity complex.

We don't have $50.00 between us. We don't have a lot of money, but we do have a lot of patience. If you will give us your full cooperation, well get the money to pay for the toll charge."

"Just because your Deputy Marshals, it doesn't mean you don't have to pay me," reasoned the store owner. "Who is this John Paul Jones character you were talking about? If he's looking for girls, why would he need a lantern? What's he doing, looking for girls after dark?"

"No, this John Paul Jones lived during The Revolutionary War. Don't you know anything about history?" asked Hannibal. "If you would be kind. If you would be so kind enough to give us a chance and wait to see what we can do. I'm sure Scooter and myself can get the money we owe you from Stephen who is the other Deputy Marshal. He will help us unravel this dramatically.

Your being foolish. Don't worry. We'll take the responsibility to pay you. It would have been better for Scooter and me to have read a book, with a nice quite western in it instead of coming into you're store. We're not going anyplace. Maybe you could, but not us."

"No, nothing doing! I don't hold with that. John Paul Jones, lanterns, looking for girls! You two are nuts!" boomed the store owner. "I don't even understand half of what you're saying! I'm going after The Marshal!"

"That's very inoculating. It looks to me like you are trying to make us feel like a trombone player with a short arm and you're putting us behind the eight ball? There is a missed delusion somewhere. Are you refusing to coordinate with me and satisticate the truth?" asked Hannibal.

"I saw what happened," Belle replied to the store owner. "Didn't you notice what happened here? It's not exactly honest what you're saying. In fact, it's a lie that this young man is responsible for breaking the lantern. That's not the point."

"What's the point?" asked the store owner. "It's not a lie. I said nothing doing. I saw him break the lantern. What's your interest in this?"

"There must be some mistake. I'll get right to the point. A word to the wise. If there is anybody to blame, I would say it was you for yelling at your customer. If you hadn't yelled at this handsome boy, he would not have dropped the lantern," answered Belle. "Go get The Marshal and I will tell him what I saw. You're the one who is forgetting. Before you get The Marshal, I will have Ace talk to you about who really caused the accident."

"You don't have to have Ace talk to me," answered the store owner. "Forget it. I'm sorry. It was all my fault that the lantern got broken. You boys don't have to pay for the lantern."

"That's more like it," laughed Belle as she went on calling Scooter by name. "Scooter, Oh Scooter."

Hearing Belle, Scooter then went on ranting, "Scooter, Oh Scooter."

"That's you stupid," laughed Hannibal. "How stupid can you be?"

"Oh! That's me. Are you talking to me lady? What did you say? I don't even know what I said," replied Scooter. "This is getting monotonous. Is there anything wrong?"

Looking at Ace, Belle said, "Look what I found." and then Belle asked Scooter, "Where did you get those beautiful blue eyes?"

"Do you mean? You don't mean? Are you sure you're talking to me? Women don't like me. I don't do good around women," Scooter replied to Belle. "Women keep asking me where I got my blue eyes. What a stupid question. Don't they know they came with the head?"

"I think your something special. How would you like to come to my office at Belle's Saloon tomorrow at 1:00 p. m. for a spot of tea?" questioned Belle.

"No, I just can't find a girl that would be interested in me, because I am always doing something stupid," explained Scooter.

"Does that mean you're not coming? You may want to reconsider. If there is anything wrong and there was something to happen, that would be part of the gamble," expressed a disappointed Belle. "I was hoping you would come. You look like a square shooter who would be a lady's man. Haven't you ever had romance with any girl?"

"You're not giving me a chance to decide," reasoned Scooter.

"I know you won't believe this. I never seem to do good around men. I don't know why. They just don't like me," insisted Belle.

"I'm beginning to appreciate you. I like you," answered Scooter. "Do you really like me?"

"Of course, I do," beamed Belle. "Everybody calls me Belle. You can call me by my first name which is Clara belle."

"That's a beautiful name," insisted Scooter. "I come from a long line of people. The name I was born with is Gomer Hickenbottom. It was given to me by my mother and father. I prefer to be called Scooter.

I am very much indebted to you. I very much want to see you and I will come tomorrow at 1:00 p. m. Right now, Hannibal and me have to get back to The Marshal's Office.

Hannibal now do you understand what I was saying about John Paul Jones. He really did know how to get a girl with a lantern. Just wait until I tell Stephen about this."

Chapter 10

I Got A Girl With A Lantern

Thirty minutes later, Stephen, Marshal Allen, Hannibal, and Scooter was sitting in The Marshal's Office eating dinner.

As everybody was sitting eating, Hannibal said to Scooter, "You sure have a lot of food on your plate. You shouldn't be eating that much. Your putting on to much weight."

Scooter answered, "Don't bother me while I'm eating. I would rather be fat and healthy than skinny and dying on my feet."

"Scooter, you know better than that. You have too many carbs and sodium on your plate," Stephen explained to Scooter. "If you don't want to be diabetic, you better lose some weight."

"What do you mean diabetic?" asked Marshal Allen.

Stephen answered The Marshal about diabetes and eating healthy. Next Stephen went on to explain what happened when he showed up at The Wilson Homestead as The Stunning Kid.

Scooter's then told of his encounter with Belle and the broken lantern. "It's just like I told you about John Paul Jones back in our Detective Office. John Paul Jones gets girls with a lantern. Now I got a girl with a lantern. Her name is Clara belle. Girls sure seem to like these lanterns. Why don't you guys get a lantern?" Scooter said to Stephen and Marshal Allen.

"What a pretty name Clara Belle has. I'm afraid that after I have that spot of tea with her tomorrow, she will not have me come back.

Whenever I try to have a romance with a girl, it never goes anywhere, because I always do something stupid. When I get around a girl, I get rattled."

"Good ole Scooter. Every girl likes to look up to the man she loves," explained Stephen. "To make sure your romance goes somewhere, you have to love her enough to lie to her. Show her that you are a lady's man. Try to be relaxed and remember your mission so you won't do anything stupid. The images you create about yourself have to be very well expressed.

Before you leave after your first date, you need to say to Clara belle, My darling girl. I very much want to see you again. Please let me take you to the Dodge City Restaurant for dinner tonight. My body trembles because I have to leave you. I want to be your devoted slave. It will be here comes the bride before you know it."

"That's a lot to remember," insisted Scooter.

"Why do you think this will work for me?"

"Never mind. You'll see after you try it." replied Stephen.

"Jumping horn toads, I have a hankering to do this. That's cowboy talk," said Scooter. "Stephen, would you write that all down for me. Then I can read it over and over, until I memorize it for tomorrow when I go to see my sweetie. I told you it was her idea that I go see her, didn't I?"

"Yes Scooter, you told me. Now I will write everything down that I told you," answered Stephen. "I'm always glad to help my friends."

Chapter 11

A Date With Belle

Finally, it was approaching 1:00 p. m. the next day and Scooter was in the saloon walking up the steps to get to Bell's Office. As Scooter reached the top of the stairs, he walked over to the office door and knocked.

"Is that you Scooter?" asked Belle.

As Scooter opened up the door, Belle said, "Come on in. Hello handsome. How nice of you to come and see me. Come and sit down on the couch by me."

"Hello Belle," said Scooter as he sat down on the couch next to Belle.

As Belle turned to face Scooter, a large spring that Belle was sitting on broke through the padding of the couch she was sitting on, pushing Belle into Scooter's lap.

"I'm sorry. This was an accident," explained Belle.

"And I thought I was going to do something stupid," blurted Scooter.

"Let's move over to the table where the hot tea is setting. I want you to call me Clara belle like all my close friends."

After Scooter and Clara belle was seated at the table, Clara belle asked, "Do you want cream and sugar in your tea?"

"No, I'll take it plain," Scooter replied.

Scooter immediately picked up the cup of tea and took a big sip of tea and then spit it out all over the table dropping the cup of tea on the table.

"Yuk, that's awful!" blurted Scooter.

"First the spring in my couch pushes me into your lap and now you don't like your tea? I feel that I'm the one doing something stupid. That is so embarrassing," cried Clara belle. "Please don't go. I'll get one of my girls to clean this up. It's fine. It's no trouble. I hope you don't leave over this. Let me get you something else. Would you like to have some vittles with me?"

"No that's OK. I just don't think I want any vittles. I would like a bottle of sarsaparilla and then can we just talk instead?" asked Scooter. "I told you I always have trouble with women. A fellow told me that moon beams and dreaming is more trouble than they are worth. I want to find out if your any different."

"I was just thinking the same thing about you," replied Clara belle. "Now you're putting the rag on the bush. As I told you, I always have trouble with men. I don't know why men don't like me. That's my problem. You really don't want to hear about my problems. I wouldn't want you to do it."

"I don't mind hearing about your problems. It's not a big deal and no trouble at all," reasoned Scooter. "You're not the only person to take a hit. The problem is not the problem. The problem is your attitude towards the problem. The only thing that is making you unhappy is your own thoughts. Tell me what this is about."

"I'm really a warm person and a terrific dancer. I always try to be friendly with men. I'm not exactly a has been. Even Ace knows that. You can make me happy," reasoned Belle.

"I used to think that the worst thing in life was to end up alone. It's not. The worst thing in life is to end up with people who make you feel alone. Everybody needs somebody, somehow. People need people. I want to find out if your different. Can't we talk and be friends?"

"I know what you mean. You still want to talk to me after I did something stupid by the mess I made?" questioned Scooter.

"I don't want you to think I'm overly concerned. I guess we both did something stupid. Life is too short to worry about stupid things.

I learned that people have to make their own mistakes. I know you're going to be alright. Have fun. Fall in love," replied Clara belle.

"I never meant a woman like you," praised Scooter. "You are the greatest."

"It's very sweet of you to say that to me," insisted Belle. "Now I really want you to stay and talk to me. It just seems right. I think you and I are making progress.

What should we talk about? I know. Tell me about this fellow Stephen Edwards. I always believed it takes a man to size up another man."

"Stephen Edwards is a man's man and he is my friend," explained Scooter. "He has iron nerve and a dead eye. He is not a bit afraid to take on a dangerous man sized job. I never saw a man that was quicker on the draw."

"Where are you and Stephen from?" asked Clara belle. "I promised myself I would never ask you that question."

"I was told not to tell anybody about Stephen, Hannibal and me," Scooter went on to say. "If I tell you about us, can I trust you not to tell anyone? I have to be careful what I do because I'm always doing something stupid."

"I'm your friend, aren't I? I just did some stupid things and you don't have to tell me if you don't want to. Asking has always come hard for me," explained Clara belle. "I want you to tell me anything. Sometimes it helps to talk. Make up any story you want, because I'm going to understand what you are saying and how you are saying it."

"If you like stories, would you like to hear the story a maid told me about a bed at a hotel I was staying at?" smiled Scooter.

"Sure, I would," answered Belle. "Oh, how fun. I could listen to your stories all day long. It's the way you put things that could really make me laugh. Tell me, what kind of a story did the maid have to tell you about a bed?"

"There really wasn't much to it, because she said she made it up," laughed Scooter. "Tell me, how do you get down from an elephant?"

"I have no idea. I have never seen an elephant," answered Belle.

"You don't get down from an elephant. You get down from a duck," laughed Scooter again. "Sometimes a laugh lightens the load and can make you happy."

"You just seem like a man I could go for and I want to know all about you. I'm sure you want me to trust you. It looks like you don't want to trust me," reasoned Belle.

"I sure can go for you as well. I think I found a woman I can trust. Unless you can get down from a duck, don't get me down," beamed Scooter.

"This is the most thrilling and exciting evening that I ever had with a man," insisted Belle.

"I've been keeping this from you long enough," insisted Scooter. "Stephen, Hannibal and myself are from Davenport, Iowa. Stephen is a professional boxer. Hannibal and I run a Detective Agency in Davenport called, The West Side Kids Detective Agency. We came back in time from April 2016"

As Scooter was talking, he stood up with an end of the tablecloth stuck in his pants. He took two steps away from the table with the tablecloth and everything on it falling to the floor. In a panic, Scooter yelled to Belle, "Listen I've got to get back to The Marshal's Office! I forgot something! I forgot to stay there! Show me one good way to get out of here and fast!" yelled Scooter as he was running out of the room, tripping over a chair, and running out the door.

"That tares it! That was really something stupid you lame brain! You bone head! You better do the old rabbit trick and get out of here!" yelled Clara belle as Scooter ran out of the room.

As Scooter ran down the stairs, Dean Dickerson was sitting at a table with his gang, in the saloon playing cards.

Chapter 12

LOOK AT THAT JASPER RUN

"We'll I'll be doggone. Something has gone haywire. Look at that jasper running down the stairs," observed Ace. "Jumping scorpions, that means Belle had a fight with him. I wonder what Belle did to him."

"Because that boy is a Deputy Marshal, it could be a grave and serious matter," reasoned Dean. "I better go up to Belle's office. I'm aiming to find out what happened."

A minute later, Dean was in Belle's office looking at the mess on the floor. "What happened Belle? What's wrong? Why are you so exited? What's all this commotion about? Did you and the Deputy Marshal have a fight?" Dean inquired.

"No, we didn't have a fight!" answered Belle. "That Deputy Marshal was right when he says he is always doing something stupid! He's a hot headed, pig headed, empty headed, deputy disaster! Some people are like clouds! Once they are gone, it's a beautiful day!"

"Simmer down. Now take a deep breath," requested Dean. "Are you loco? He can't be as bad as that. Not by a long shot. He hasn't been here long enough for you not to like him."

"Don't you understand me? It was a lousy idea to begin with. I couldn't believe what I was seeing. I can't believe how one man can be involved in so many incidents," explained Belle.

"What's this all about? What was he doing?" asked Dean.

"You wouldn't believe me if I told you," replied Belle.

"Hog wash. Was it really that bad?" gasped Dean. "Didn't you find anything out from him at all?"

"May I continue? That's what I call a simple minded man who has some stupid idea about being happy. He sure doesn't have to make an effort to get into trouble, because he was already driving me up the wall the minute he got here. He is probably the biggest nut I've ever seen. After I tell you what happened, you will think I was crazy for doing this.

The first thing that happened was after he took a sip of my good tea, he spit it all out on the table and knocked his cup over with the rest of the tea in it. Then the tablecloth was caught in his pants and when he stood up everything on the table came crashing to the floor. I was so mad. In made me upset, really upset. Then I started yelling at him and he ran off every which way. Now you see what I mean?"

"Oh, he did, did he? I can't believe it. That sounds incredible. What a shock it must have been to see it. Before that happened, did you find anything out from The Deputy what Stephen Edwards was planning to do?" asked Dean. "I sure hope that clumsy idiot didn't get wise. He was our one chance to find out what we needed to know about this Stephen Edwards."

"I feel sorry for that lovable, misguided Scooter in a way. All that trouble for nothing. I needed more time with him," noted Belle. "We'll never find someone else with a brain like his.

All I could find out from him was that Stephen Edwards and the other two Deputies are from Davenport, Iowa. Stephen is a professional boxer and the other two clowns run a Detective Agency. Then he told me the strangest thing that's hard to believe. As he was starting to stand up, he said the three of them are from the year 2016."

"That's the worst story I ever heard. Are you sure he said that? You can't be serious?" reasoned Dean. "Now that's it's over with, what are you going to do next?"

"With his mentality, it's hard to say," replied Belle. "I'll have to find a way to get him back to my office and try something else. After he serves his purpose, we'll get rid of him. There are more ways to skin a rattler.

There is a big payroll shipment coming in by stage later today. I just heard about it and I want a chance to get my hands on that money. It sure beats working your fingers to the bone. Take the boys and get that money. You will have to set a trap because there will be an army escort."

"If this Stunning Kid shows up, I'm also going to get rid of him?" replied Dean.

"I don't want you to tell me about it. I want you to do it. Dig another grave for him," answered Belle. "I want that money. I have plans for it."

As Belle was talking to Dean about holding up the stage, Scooter was back in The Marshal's Office telling about his visit to Clara belle.

Chapter 13

I really thought Clara belle Was For Me

"I really thought Clara belle was the woman for me and I am plumb out of my scull about her," Scooter went on to say. "When I went up to her office to see her, she invited me to sit on a couch next to her. She kept touching me like she couldn't believe I was real. She just kept coming and coming at me and I got all stoked up about her. Then a spring in the couch that she was sitting on came through the couch and pushed her in my lap.

Then I really did some stupid things. After she gave me a cup of tea to drink, I took a sip. It tasted so awful that I spit it out all over the table and knocked my cup over.

Then somehow the tablecloth got tucked in my pants. When I stood up from the table, I pulled the tablecloth off the table with the dishes on it and they all came crashing to the floor.

I can't face Belle anymore. It's no use. There is just no pleasing that girl. I thought she was starting to love me. I think I made a mistake to go see her. Now I have a broken heart and nothing to live for. What can I do to fix this or does this prove I can't fix being stupid?"

"It's very simple," replied Stephen. "None of us can stay here in this time period. We came here to do a job and then go home. I think you

49

should give some serious thought about finding another girl. When we get back home, Hannibal and I will help you find the right woman."

"Is there a woman who will put up with me every time I do something stupid?" questioned Scooter.

"Yes Scooter. You are really a good person and fun to be around," reasoned Stephen. "The right woman will go out of their way to make it obvious that she wants you in her life and she's will be a keeper. She will put up with you every time you do something stupid. In fact, she will never even notice if you do anything stupid. If she can make you mad but happy, that's euphoria."

"Stephen has that right," broke in Hannibal. "If a woman says that looks and brains aren't important in your case, it's her way of saying she loves you."

"Hannibal, stop it," demanded Stephen. "Don't say things like that to Scooter. He feels bad enough about what happened. Scooter is our friend and I'm trying to help him."

"I know it," reasoned Hannibal. "I've always treated Scooter that way. It isn't like it sounds because Scooter has always been like a brother to me."

"I understand that. Unless you have something nice to say that is helpful, keep quiet," instructed Stephen. "Now Scooter, I have something very important to tell you.

Life is too short, and happiness is so rare. If there is ever a slight chance of finding a woman who will make you happy, risk it, because she's a keeper.

Remember, knowing yourself is the beginning of all wisdom. Living a life avoiding doing something stupid does only one thing for you. It never gives you the opportunity to see what you really can do. You need to choose honesty over perfection every time, then have the ability to adapt and overcome. Failure will only build your character.

If you've got nothing going for you today, you need to get yourself together. Now is the time to make up your mind to be sure you're right and then go ahead, because you want to make sure all the good times aren't slipping away. Smile, grow, want, crave, feel, always make every minute count.

Some days you have to rise above the storm, and you will find the sunshine. Sometimes we need fantasy to survive the reality. Be silly. Be fun. Every time you find some humor in a difficult situation, create your own sunshine.

To do that, make your own kind of music. Remember, a smile is king and then begin to sing and make it groovy even if nobody sings along with you. Be different. Be you because life is too short to be anything but happy and you will win.

One of the best lessons you can learn in life is trying to master how to remain calm. The happiest people don't have the best of everything. They just make the best of everything they have.

If you want to tell people the truth, be crazy and make them laugh, otherwise they will get very mad at you. A positive attitude may not solve all of your problems, but it will annoy enough people to make it worth the effort. It's your life. Don't ever let anyone make you feel guilty for living life your way.

Everyone is your friend until you ask them for a favor. If you ask me how long I will be your friend, my answer will be, I don't know how long I'll be your friend, because I really don't know which one is longer, forever or always.

I have a motto I go by that I've been wanting to tell you.

Scooter, try and remember this:

Good people give you happiness.

Bad people give you experience.

The worst people give you a lesson.

The best people give you memories.

If you have a better way of going,

you better show me how.

Now is not the time and place to be distracted by a woman and doing stupid things. Worrying about that may just get you killed. You came here to help me because you are my friend. As your friends, I give you my word. When we get back home, Hannibal and I will find you somebody," explained Stephen as the Bank President came rushing through the door.

Chapter 14
The Payroll Shipment

"Marshal, Marshal Allen. I just got a telegram that a large payroll shipment is coming by stage, with an army escort to be put in my bank," said The Bank President. "Would you and your Deputies go meet the stage and help escort it into Dodge?"

"How soon will it be here?" asked Marshal Allen.

"It's on its way now and if you don't hurry, it may not get here at all," replied The Bank President.

"OK boys. Now I need you. Let's go to the stable and get our horses," ordered Marshal Allen.

"O boy, now I get to be a cowboy like Roy Rogers," exclaimed Scooter.

"I would rather be like John Wayne, pilgrim," added Hannibal.

"Who is this Roy Rogers and John Wayne?" asked Marshal Allen.

"Never mind. We'll tell you about them when we get back. I just want to get to the stables and get Lightning saddled," beamed Stephen. "As dangerous as this is going to be, it still sounds like a lot of fun. This is just the kind of thing you would see in a movie. Now I get to do it."

After our heroes saddled their horses, they rode out of town on the south road. Thirty minutes later, they approached the stage that was stopped in the middle of the road. All four of the army escort had been shot and killed. The driver and guard was sitting on top of the stage badly wounded. There were no passengers.

Stephen quickly bandaged the driver and guard using his first aid knowledge from the 21st century.

"Stephen, you take the stage into town and find the doctor for these two," instructed Marshal Allen. "Hannibal and Scooter can stay here and help me bury the army escort. I think you better pay Dean Dickerson a visit."

As Stephen pulled up to the stage depot, he yelled, "The stage has been robbed. Find the doctor for the stage driver and guard."

He then jumped off the stage on to Lightning and headed to the stable, where he quickly changed his clothes to become The Stunning Kid. After he saddled Thunder, he rode Thunder out of the back of the stables over behind Belle's Saloon. Looking through the window of Dean Dickerson's Office, The Stunning Kid watched Dean open up his safe. As Dean was crouched down putting the stolen money from the stage in his safe, The Stunning Kid came through the back door to Dean's Office with his gun drawn.

"Hand over that money you took from holding up the stage and put it all in my saddle bags," ordered The Stunning Kid. "While we're at it, give me all the money you have in your safe."

"So, you're The Stunning Kid. I've been wanting to meet you," muttered Dean. "I have been wanting to talk to you about working together in this territory."

"It looks like we are already working together. You saved me a lot of time and trouble by taking the money off the stage," replied The Stunning Kid. "We already have a fine arrangement. You and your gang does the dirty work, robbing stages and chasing homesteaders off their land. I get the money and you get blamed for it.

Just a word of caution. I'm only going to tell you once. All this land you been stealing around here is mine now. Give back the land you took to the homesteaders and don't be forcing any more homesteaders off of their land. I have a purpose of my own to let them live on their property."

Just as The Stunning Kid was ready to leave, Lefty, Danny, Mugs and Shorty came through the back door of the office.

"Reach for the sky you viper," ordered Lefty with his gun drawn.

"My men are here. What are you doing here? Maybe you think you can blow out the sun with one puff, but you'll never get out of here," Dean said to The Stunning Kid. "Unmask him."

"What's the use? It's got to come sooner or later," answered The Stunning Kid who immediately turned around knocking the gun out of Lefty's hand with the saddle bags and pushed Lefty into Danny, Mugs and Shorty. He then rushed out the front door of the office into the saloon with the saddle bags over his left shoulder with both guns drawn.

"Don't anybody move," ordered The Stunning Kid as he ran out of the front door and jumped on the back of an empty buckboard that was parked in front of the saloon. Standing up in the back behind the seats of the buckboard, he grabbed the reins and yelled, "Yah! Yah!" and the team of horses started running down the street. After going about 200 feet, The Stunning Kid jumped off the buckboard in front of The General Store as the horses continued to run.

He ran up the outside stairs connected to The General Store as Lefty, Danny, Shorty, and Mugs ran after him. When The Stunning Kid reached the top of the stairs, he climbed on top of the railing and then pulled himself up on the roof.

"There he is!" yelled Danny as he pulled his revolver and fired, missing The Stunning Kid.

The Stunning Kid ran across the roof tops toward Belle's Saloon. As he reached Belle's saloon, he walked to the edge of the roof that was above Dean's Office and jumped off, landing on Thunder and rode away.

"OK boys. Let's hit leather. Get your horses and go after him!" yelled Dean as he ran out the front door of the saloon in a rage.

Fifteen minutes later as The Stunning Kid was riding out of town on a dirt road, he approaches some trees. As he rides under one of the trees, he reaches up with a rope in one of his hands and grabs a limb to the tree hanging over the road. He pulls himself up over the limb and then stands on the limb crouching. Then he yells, "Thunder go hide!"

Within seconds, Lefty and Danny ride under the limb followed by Shorty and Mugs. As The Stunning Kid has one end of the rope tied to the limb, he throws the loop of the other end of the rope over

Shorty and Mugs. Shorty and Mugs are now hanging in midair as the rope is now around their chests and under their arms.

The Stunning Kid jumps off the limb and runs over to mount Thunder. He races after Lefty and Danny. As he catches up to Lefty and Danny who is riding side by side, he transfers to Danny's horse, pushing Danny over to Lefty knocking the three of them on the ground. The Stunning Kid quickly stands up and pulls out one of his revolvers telling Lefty and Danny to stand up.

"Take your guns out of your holsters with their thumbs and forefingers and throw them on the ground," ordered The Stunning Kid. "Now get back on your horses and ride back to Shorty and Mugs."

As the three men ride up to Shorty and Mugs, they are still hanging from the tree limb.

"Get off you horses and cut them down," ordered The Stunning Kid.

As the four men are now standing before The Stunning Kid, he tells them to take their boots off and throw them in the weeds.

"Now start walking back to town," demanded The Stunning Kid as he fires a warning shot into the ground and the four men begin running away from The Stunning Kid.

Chapter 15

The Adventure of The Stolen Payroll

Fifteen minutes later The Stunning Kid is firing his guns in the air as he rides Thunder at a gallop down the street towards The Marshal's Office.

In seconds he is in front of The Marshal's Office and he throws the saddle bags full of stolen money in front of the door to The Marshal's Office.

"Come on out Marshal," yelled The Stunning Kid and then he rode away.

As the Marshal opens up the door and as he looked down at the saddle bags, he sees a note attached to the saddle bags. After The Marshal picked up the saddle bags, he stood there and read the note that said, "Here is the money taken off the stage, Compliments of The Stunning Kid."

"Come here Hannibal and Scooter," ordered The Marshal. "The Stunning Kid just returned the money that was taken off the stage. That's what I call getting justice from outside the law. Isn't that nice. Just like downtown. I need both of you to go with me as guards, to take this money to the bank."

Fifteen minutes later, Stephen returned to The Marshal's Office where Scooter, Hannibal and The Marshal was enjoying a cup of coffee and talking about the stage hold up.

"Stephen, It's about time you got back. In fact, we could hardly wait for you to come back," said an excited Marshal Allen. "We want to know how The Stunning Kid got the money back from the stage holdup?"

Stephen then explained to everyone how The Stunning Kid went to Dean Dickerson's Office and took the money by gunpoint while Dean had the safe open. He then went on to tell everyone how Lefty and the boys surprised him when they came in the back door behind him with their guns drawn.

"I thought Lefty had me for a minute," said Stephen. "I think what saved me was being able to think fast though my training and experience in boxing."

Next Stephen told of his escape and being chased by The Dean Dickerson Gang. As he finished his story about how he captured the gang and then made them walk back to town without their boots, he went on to say,

"That was a dandy ride. I couldn't believe I had it in me to do what I did. What excitement! What an adventure! If I didn't know any better, I would think this was a dream. As The Stunning Kid, I got the ball rolling in putting this gang out of business."

"What's next?" broke in Marshal Allen.

Chapter 16

MARKSMANSHIP PRACTICE

"I don't know what anybody else is going to do next," interrupted Scooter. "I'm going down behind the stable and practice my marksmanship. Hannibal, did you notice if there are any bulls eyes in the back of our wagon?"

"They're in a box behind the seat," answered Hannibal. "I'm going to stay here and find out what were going to do next. Be careful so you don't shoot yourself or someone else."

"What do you think I'm going to do, something stupid?" replied Scooter as he was going out the door. A few seconds later Scooter came back through the door again saying, "Oops I almost did something stupid. I better take my gun with me."

Ten minutes later Scooter was behind the stable, attaching a bull's eye to a bale of hay. He then walked fifteen feet away from the target. As Scooter started shooting at the bull's eye, Stephen was watching from the back door of the stable. Scooter hit a saddle hanging on a fence, the bell in the church steeple, one of the hinges on the gate and knocked the hat off of Stephen's head.

"What are you doing?" scolded Stephen to Scooter. "Make up your mind. Whose side are you on?"

"I'm sorry Stephen. I wouldn't hurt you for anything," cried Scooter. "If I'm going to be a Deputy Marshal, I've got to practice my marksmanship, don't I?"

"It's my fault. I shouldn't be taking unnecessary chances standing here while your practicing," replied Stephen. "The least you could do is to try to hit what you're aiming at. Next time go easy on the trigger. Come back to The Marshal's Office. I have a job for you."

Chapter 17

THE POKER GAME

Ten minutes later, in The Marshal's Office Stephen was giving Scooter instructions about going to Belle's Saloon.

"Ace and the boys are probably in the saloon playing poker," Stephen said to Scooter. "I want you to take these hundred dollar bills and get in that poker game. Every time you open, bet $100.00 no matter what your cards look like."

"Ace is a poor looser. No matter how much he loses, Ace won't quit," explained Marshal Allen. "Were hoping Ace will bet one of those $100.00 counterfeit bills and you'll win the pot."

"I don't know how to play poker. How can I win a pot?" replied Scooter. "I don't know how to talk western talk. What if Ace gets mad at me?"

"Just act natural. I can promise you that Ace won't," explained Stephen.

"Stephen, that's bad advice your giving to Scooter. You know better to tell him that. If Scooter acts natural, Ace is sure to get mad at him," replied Hannibal.

"Scooter don't worry about Ace. Stephen, The Marshal, and yours truly will be there to keep an eye on you. Just do what The Marshal says, and you will win a pot. We're going to be there to help you and we're not going to let anybody hurt you."

"I know you're trying to protect me. OK, since Stephen taught me a little bit about boxing, I'll do it," answered Scooter. "I'm very nervous about this. Let's go now and get it over with before I change my mind."

Five minutes later all four lawmen was in Belle's Saloon.

"There they are Scooter. Ace and his buddies are playing poker. Go get in the game and try to win some money," urged Stephen.

"Good afternoon gentlemen. Nice day. Nice day. This looks like this is going to be the day," laughed Scooter.

"Says who?" demanded Ace.

"Says me. I really like to play poker. It's a fine game," stated Scooter.

"Says who?" repeated Ace.

"Is this a private game or do you mind if I sit in?" asked Scooter.

"If you would like to join us, sit down," ordered Ace.

"Says who?" questioned Scooter.

"Says me," roared Ace.

"You don't say. Well howdy buckaroos," replied Scooter as he sat down. "That's cowboy talk."

"Lefty go ahead and deal," ordered Ace.

After Ace picked up his cards to see what he had, he said, "I'll open for $3.00."

"I'll bet $100.00," said Scooter as he put a $100.00 bill in the pot.

"I thought we were just going to have friendly bets. Who is this man? What's he doing here?" asked an anxious Danny. "How can he bet $100.00 when he didn't even look at his cards?"

"It isn't for me to say," replied Ace.

"Says who?" broke in Scooter.

"Says me," answered Ace.

"Is that so?" added Scooter.

"I've got to stay. I would be a fool to pass this up," insisted Ace. "If that's how you want to play poker, this is my chance to make some money."

"Says who?' asked Scooter.

"Says me," replied Ace.

"I'm out," said Danny as he got up to leave. "That's too rich for my blood."

"I'm out," said Shorty.

"Me too," said Mugs.

"You guys give up so easily. I need to put the pressure on him. I'm going to go and hit him hard. I want that pot," insisted Ace. "When the pressure is on, that's when I'm at my best. Here's my $100.00 and I will raise you $100.00."

"If you're staying, I'm staying," replied Lefty. "Here's my $200.00."

Looking over at Stephen, who was holding two fingers up, Scooter pondered a minute."

"What are you doing?" asked Ace.

"Just thinking," replied Scooter.

"Don't think too hard. It might give you nightmares," laughed Ace.

"Here's my $100.00 and I raise you $200.00," Scooter decided to say.

"That settles it for me. I'm out," snorted Lefty.

"You win the pot. What did you have?" questioned Ace.

"It's hard to say. Let me look," replied Scooter as he pulled the money from the pot in front of him. "This looks like a good haul and should be easy to count with just $100.00 bills in the pot."

"Get a load of super genius playing cards," observed Hannibal.

"I know," replied Stephen. "I gave him the ideas and he is getting the credit. Even though he's acting natural, at least he is using his head."

"Wait a minute. What were you doing?" asked Ace. "You mean to say you bet all that money and you didn't know what you had?"

"I can't say," replied Scooter.

"So you think that is a cleaver conception on how to play poker? I thought you was just bluffing," reasoned Ace.

"I can't say because it's hard to say. Don't you trust me?" asked Scooter.

"I can't say. I just don't like to play games," answered Ace.

"That's just the way I bet when I play poker," explained Scooter.

"Says who?" questioned Ace.

"Says me," answered Scooter. "Let's see. I have a 3 of spades, a 5 of clubs, a red jack and a black queen and a 10 of diamonds."

"Why you cheap tin horn! I'm going to get my money back, in a hurry!" shouted Ace. "Deal the cards again. This time it's going to be just you and me playing poker."

"Says who?" asked Scooter.

"Says me!" shouted Ace. "I don't know how you came up with this idea to play poker!"

"I can't say!" shouted Scooter.

"What have you been eating, locoweed? I ought to cut you into little pieces and feed you to the buzzards!" yelled Ace."

"You don't say. Some people are so touchy. You can make a man deaf yelling like that.

You aren't any different than Rex when I blew up his new car and the Dean when I broke his expensive statue twice all in one day. Next time you play cards, carry your brain with you," replied Scooter. "Now that I won some money, I'm done playing cards."

"Wait a minute. Don't I get a chance to get my money back?" demanded Ace.

"What can I do for you? I'll tell you what. I'll give you a chance to make your money back and you won't have to play poker to get it," volunteered Scooter. "I was saving this for last."

"Just what do I have to do to get my money back?" roared Ace.

"I will bet $200.00, double or nothing and I'll prove you're not here," explained Scooter.

"That should be a sure thing for me. I'll take that bet. This is going to be simple," replied Ace.

"We shall see what we will see," laughed Scooter.

"This should be interesting. Prove to me that I'm not here," demanded Ace.

"Before we bet, would you have a five for two tens?" asked Scooter.

"Ace is sure falling for this one," Scooter said to himself.

"I sure do," replied Ace. "Now you're talking."

"I said that wrong," laughed Scooter. "Give me back my five and I'll give you back your two tens."

"I almost blew that one," Scooter said to himself.

"You've got it," roared Ace. "Now prove to me that I'm not here."

"I've got this one made in the shade. This is not even going to be a challenge. We all know that your lights are on and that there is nobody home," laughed Scooter.

"What do you mean that you have this made in the shade? Back up and start again. You're in the saloon, not outside where all that fresh air is. And what's this wise crack about my lights are on and there is nobody home?" snarled Ace. "Are you making fun of me?"

"Why Ace, would I do that to you? After I win this bet, it will prove that I have this made in the shade and that your lights are on and there is nobody home.

OK, you put your money where your mouth is. You put your money on the table, and I'll put my money on the table.

Observe, listen closely. This requires a great deal of skill and intelligence which you are short of. Now I will test your skill so you can prove to me that you' re here and not someplace else. If you can, you will be handsomely rewarded, and I will pay you the entire amount. That should cheer you up if that happens.

Here it goes. Tell me, are you in St. Louis?"

"No, I'm not in St. Louis," answered Ace.

"Are you in Chicago?" asked Scooter.

"Of course not. How can I be in Chicago?" asked Ace.

"Then how about California?" questioned Scooter.

"No, I'm not in California or Chicago, or St' Louis. "It's a lie. You can see that I'm not in any of those places, so I get the money," insisted Ace.

"Hold on. I have some bad news for you. You yourself said that you're not in California, Chicago or St Louis. That means you must be someplace else. If your someplace else, you can't be here. I won the bet. Wasn't I clever?" insisted Scooter as he reached over to pick up the money.

"I think I'm going to let you have it by whaling the dickens out of you!" yelled Ace.

"What else? Why you Tale of Two Cities, You Oliver Twist, You David Copperfield!" yelled Scooter.

"What are you chattering about now?" growled Ace. "Do you have to do that?"

"I just gave you The Dickens. How do you like that?" asked Scooter as Belle was walking down the stairs from her office.

"I have been playing poker a long time with great conversation with other people. I haven't had an intelligent conversation with you yet!" screamed Ace.

"As I said before, your lights are on and there is nobody home!" roared Scooter. "Because you're a nerd, you talk too much and don't even have a friendly smile. I don't think you have had any intelligent conversations in weeks or even months.

I'm only responsible for what I say to you, not what you think you understand what I said. You're always lost in thought and that unfamiliar territory with you. I see what the problem is here. I'm talking in English and you listen as if you were a moron. What you lack in intelligence, you make up for in ignorance."

"Listen to Scooter go," said Stephen to Hannibal. "Those are things I said to him about dealing with Belle and other people.

Remember when I told him if he wants to tell people the truth, make them laugh, otherwise they will get very mad at you. Now he's unloading it all on Ace and Ace isn't laughing.

I also told him that a positive attitude may not solve all of his problems, but it will upset enough people to make it worth the effort. He better watch his step as to what he is saying to Ace, because Ace is beginning to be annoyed and Ace means business."

"We better keep an eye on Ace. He may not take this too kindly," replied Marshal Allen. "Ace will attack you and you will feel like your wrestling with a gorilla. You don't stop when you're done. You stop when Ace is done."

"Those are very deleterious statements that Scooter is making to Ace. Stephen, it's a good thing you're a professional undefeated boxer," beamed Hannibal. "You have the self-offense of a roaring tiger and your able to lick your weight in gorillas. I've seen you use your magic punch on Ace.

I'm not worried about Ace. He is always trying to put salt on our tails by brewing up some trouble, because he is a work of art. I've seen you go toe to toe with Ace using the manly art of self-offense and he always falls for your sucker punch and you've knocked him down a couple of times."

"It's just plain pitiful," Scooter went on to say, "Because I feel like a fool talking to you. Life is hard enough. I never argue with an idiot because life is even harder when you're stupid. People watching and listening to the argument won't be able to tell the difference as to which one of us is the idiot. My advice to you is to quite being yourself or you're always going to stay weird."

"So, I don't handle people as well as you. It makes no never mind to me. For a little guy, you talk like a big man. No one treats me like that. No one," roared Ace as he pulled his revolver out of his holster and set it on the table. "You have a big mouth and you're talking about me and then laughing at me. It's time for you and me to have a hoopty do. You say that one more time and I'll bust you in the nose Then let's see how capable you are at taking care of yourself."

"Consider it said," replied Scooter.

"Consider it busted," answered Ace.

"That's telling him Ace," broke in Hannibal.

Chapter 18

SCOOTER WOULD YOU COME TO MY OFFICE AGAIN?

"Ace, if Scooter isn't capable of taking care of himself, I am capable of taking care of him! Mind your manners! Leave that boy alone! You have been celebrating too much! You're as drunk as a skunk!" screamed Belle. "We'll talk about this tomorrow!

Scooter, will you come up to my office again? I won't yell at you anymore. I just want to talk to you. This time I will have the bartender bring up a bottle of sarsaparilla for you."

Scooter immediately looked over at Stephen who was shaking his head yes.

"Are you sure you just want to talk to me again?" asked Scooter.

"Yes Scooter. Please come up to my office," replied Belle.

"Alright, I'll come up and talk to you again. I'll be right there. At least it's worth a try. Here we go again."

Looking at Ace, Scooter then said, "See you later Alligator."

"Scooter, before you go upstairs, do you have something to give us?" asked Stephen.

"Oh, the money from the poker game. Look what I won. Here, take it," offered Scooter.

Two minutes later, Scooter was again walking through the door to Belle's office.

"Oh Scooter, what a delightful surprise. I'm very anxious to talk to you and I want to really thank you for giving me a second chance to talk to you," Belle went on to say. "We don't seem to be having much going for us. I think you're the one man I can get to like. I just hope you feel the same way about me."

"I do feel the same way about you," answered Scooter.

"I want you to know that you really broke my heart when you ran out of my office. It was so degrading," explained Belle. "It's not because you pulled the tablecloth off the table, with the dishes falling on the floor breaking them into pieces or even what you said. It's what you did after that."

"What did I do?" asked Scooter.

"It's not what you did. It's how you did it running away from me like a scared rabbit, tripping over the chair as you ran out," muttered Belle.

"I ran out of here because I was so embarrassed that I did something stupid and you were too busy finding faults in me while I was too busy overlooking yours," replied Scooter.

"When I pulled the tablecloth off of the table and the dishes went crashing to the floor, it scared twenty pounds off of me. That's why I don't get along with women because I keep doing things that are stupid."

"I never meant the things I said when I yelled at you as you ran out of my office. That's not my idea of friendship," replied Belle. "Let's be friends. Let's have it understood that I promise I'll be good.

Everybody has bad days and does something stupid. It's OK not to be OK. It's not going to be as bad as all of that. You seem to have your share of bad days. Some days are just harder than others.

That is one of the things that makes me so attracted to you. My mind says don't do it. Don't fall in love with you, but my heart says yes. You are a one of a kind, shy clean cut man with that crooked nose that I'm attracted to. Can you ever forgive me?"

"You just flatter me to pieces." answered Scooter. "You are the prettiest saloon owner I've ever seen. The Marshal and his posse could never make me leave this town after seeing you.

Do you really mean you like me? If that is so, I can be just me when I'm with you. I don't have to worry about doing something stupid. Stephen Edwards and Hannibal are my friends because they don't get mad at me when I do something stupid.

You may think this is a fairy tale. I have some more friends at home that work with Hannibal and me in our Detective Agency. Now let's see," said Scooter as he was counting on his fingers, "There is Who, What, I Don't Know, You Don't Say, Whatever, I'm Not Sure, Smiley and Because."

"What kind of names are those? I never heard of names like that before," questioned Belle.

"Oh, those were nicknames that was given to our friends when we started our baseball team and they kept them ever since.

On the bases we had Who on first, What on second and I Don't Know on third."

"What's a baseball team and what are bases?" asked Belle "Who were these people?"

"Only one of these people was Who. The other two I mentioned was What and I Don't Know. You believe me, don't you?" questioned Scooter as he took the coin out of his pocket that Don gave him and flipped it in the air repeatedly catching it.

"Wait a minute. You mean to say that you had what you called was a ball team and you didn't know the names of three people on the team?" asked Belle.

"I just told you their names and the name of our baseball team was called The West Side Kids," explained Scooter. "After we all graduated from high school, Hannibal formed a club called The West Side Kids. We all have Wild Indian Motorcycles and leather jackets with our nick names and the name of the club on them."

"What's a motorcycle?" asked Belle as Ace entered the office. "Even though I don't understand it all, it was a very interesting story and I'm glad you told me.

Ace, how many times have I told you to knock when the door is closed? Ace get out of here. You're going to spoil everything. We would like to be alone."

Chapter 19
ACE VISITS THE 21ST CENTURY

As Scooter flipped his coin in the air again, Ace caught it. A couple seconds later, Ace disappeared moving forward through time to the 21st century.

"How did Ace do that?" exclaimed Scooter. "He disappeared just like Stephen did when we went after The Jerry Dickerson Gang."

A couple seconds later, Ace appeared again. Only it was in Rex's Office at The Davenport Police Department. There sat Rex at his desk while his brother Don stood by a table where his time machine set.

"Where am I? Who are you guys?" demanded Ace as he dropped the coin out of his hand and pulled his revolver out of his holster.

"There is nothing to be frightened about," answered Rex.

"We just had a little mix up and were going to send you back home."

As Ace looked around, he saw a television setting on a filling cabinet tuned into a Chicago Cubs ball game. He then looked out the window facing 4th street with cars driving by. Next, he looked at a newspaper sitting on the table by the time machine. The date was April 30, 2016. The headline read, "US Strikes In Afghanistan Extend Far Beyond White House Claims."

With a frightened look on his face Ace asked again as he pointed his gun at Rex, "Who are you guys and where am I?"

"I might as well tell you. Nobody is going to believe you when you go back home," explained Rex. "Put that gun away. If you kill my brother Don and me, you will never get back home. That is a time machine on the table. This time machine transports people through time, and it will get you back home. My brother and I are the only ones that know how it works. We also need to find that coin that fell out of your hand. You will need that to get back home. That coin belonged to Scooter. How did you get it?"

"That idiot. Is he for real? He's so stupid, he couldn't hit the ground with his hat," growled Ace. "When I entered Belle's Office, he flipped the coin that fell on the floor in the air and I caught it. The next thing I know, I'm here."

"We're going to send you back home," explained Rex. "I strongly suggest that you when you get back that you give this coin back to Scooter. This doing something stupid is just an act that he puts on. Scooter is really the leader and brains of The West Side Kids Detective Agency here in Davenport, Iowa.

Steven Edwards and Hannibal are actually working for him. He can be very tough and even a killer. When he starts to shiver all over, you and everybody around you better take cover somewhere because you never know what he is going to do next."

"I thought there was something funny about him," reasoned Ace.

"Now put that gun away and sit in that chair. Wait right here and don't move. My name is Detective Rex Tarillo and this is my brother Don Tarillo who invented that time machine. While Don is looking for that coin you dropped on the floor, I wonder if I can have a talk with you? Let's chew the fat and have a drink. We don't have to bother anybody.

You are at The Davenport Police Station and as you may have read in the paper on the table, the date is April 30, 2016. There are several police officers in this building. If you try anything stupid, you will be arrested and put in jail. You will never get home."

Ace then put his gun back into his holster and sat down saying to Rex, "Tell me. Am I in a dream? You're not a real person, are you? What do you want to know?"

"I guess you can say that you're in a dream and I'm not a real person, so it's OK to tell me what I want to know. After you do that, you will be sent home and you can wake up. I want to know about Dean Dickerson and everything he's in to," explained Rex. "What part do you play in his gang?"

"I guess I'm in a dream. Everything I see around me can't be real," reasoned Ace as he explained to Rex everything he wanted to know.

After Rex was satisfied what Ace told him, he handed Ace the coin and Don hit the button on the time machine.

After Ace disappeared, Rex informed Don that he had to call Columbo and have him come to his office. Columbo was not at the Police Station and it was thirty minutes before Columbo arrived at Rex's Office. Rex told Columbo about talking to Ace after he appeared in his office.

"Columbo, after talking to Ace I think the boys can use our help," explained Rex. "Now that we know that we can bring them back home, would you be interested in going back in time with the rest of The West Side Kids and me to help them out? I'm looking forward to meeting my great, great, great grandfather, Rocky Allen."

"That's right. If I go back in time, I will get to meet my great, great, great grandfather, Oliver Columbo. This would be a very interesting assignment and it would be nice to get away for a while," replied Columbo. "I'm starting to miss the boys. I'll do it."

"OK, let's put in for immediate vacation time," suggested Rex. "Next we need to contact The West Side Kids and give them a crash course in fire arms and horses."

In seconds Ace was back in Belle's Office as if he never disappeared from Belle and Scooter's sight.

"Here Scooter. I didn't mean to take your coin," offered Ace. "Belle, I'm going back to my poker game. I don't even remember why I came to your office."

As Ace started to leave, Belle said to him, "This may sound crazy to you. It seems like you just disappeared out of sight for a couple of seconds."

"I don't know how you got that idea," relied Ace. "Maybe you have been dreaming or have you had too much to drink."

"No, I haven't!" yelled Belle. "You're the one who has had to much to drink! After you come to your senses, tell Dean to come up to my office after Scooter leaves."

Chapter 20

GRUBSTAKE

As Ace came down the stairs from Belle's Office, A bearded prospector, named Grubstake came into the saloon yelling, "I found it! I found it! I struck gold, Santana's gold! Now I have to take a bath that I'm rich!"

Because of what the prospector said, Stephen quickly left the saloon and disappeared. Hearing Grubstake yelling, Scooter and Belle walked out of Belle's office to the top of the stairs.

"I wouldn't take a bath if I were you. The shock might kill you," replied Ace. "Are you sure you struck gold this time? The last time you struck gold, you was put in jail for striking Sheriff Gold at Twin Forks."

"I tell you I found it. Of course, I found it," answered Grubstake.

"Are you sure this isn't Sheriff Santana's Gold that you struck?" asked Ace.

"I found the real thing. I'm rich I tell you," replied Grubstake.

"If this is the real thing, I'm going to have a talk with you. You better tell me where you found the gold or your life won't be worth a plug nickel," threatened Ace.

"I'm not going to tell you," said Grubstake. "I was so excited when I found gold, that after years of looking I just wanted to tell everybody," roared Grubstake. "I never should have said anything about striking it rich. You will never find out from me where my treasure is."

Ace then grabbed Grubstake by the shirt and said as he was raising his fist,

"I asked you a question. Maybe you need some help to loosen your tongue," insisted Ace.

"Leave Grubstake alone," ordered Marshal Allen as he walked up to Ace.

Dean, Lefty, Danny, Shorty, and Mugs stood up from their chairs where they were playing poker and walked behind Ace pulling their guns out of their holsters.

"Are these lawmen friends of yours?" Danny asked the prospector.

"I don't know who these men are and what they're doing here except for Marshal Allen," answered Grubstake.

"Grubstake, where is your gold mine?" asked Ace again. "Start talking."

"How can I talk with guns north and the south of me?" roared Grubstake.

"Marshal, I think it's time you and your two Deputies took a walk," ordered Dean. "I don't want any rough stuff in my saloon."

The Marshal looked around for Stephen and he was gone.

"We'll skin the hide off of you if you don't leave now," insisted Dean as The Stunning Kid came through the front door of the saloon with both guns drawn.

"Well brand my britches. Do you know who that is?" asked one of the customers to the bartender.

"It's The Stunning Kid!" answered the bartender as he pulled a shot gun from behind the bar, aiming it at The Stunning Kid saying, "This is the end of the trail for you."

It just an instant The Stunning Kid aimed one of his guns at the bartender, shooting the shotgun out of his hands.

"I've got two guns. One for each of you. Everyone else holster your hardware or I'm going to finish the job," ordered The Stunning Kid.

"Nobody called you in on this play. Why are you here?" asked Dean. "How did you find out about the prospector's gold so fast? Are you after his gold?"

"That's my business to find out about the gold. I want his gold the same as you and your boys," answered The Stunning Kid. "You know how it is when a fellow gets broke and hungry. I told you and your boys before that Dodge City is now my territory."

"I am having wanted posters made up for your capture," said The Marshal to The Stunning Kid.

"I'll tell you what Marshal. You don't bother me, and I won't bother you," replied The Stunning Kid. "Alright old timer, you come with me and we will find a nice quite place to talk about your gold."

"Marshal, Marshal help me. Don't you dare let anybody steel my gold," pleaded Grubstake. "I don't want to go with this masked bandit. Ain't it your job to protect folks?"

"There is nothing I can do with those two colt 45s pointed at me," observed The Marshal. "I don't think he will hurt you if you go without a fight. As soon as Stephen Edwards hears about this, he will rescue you."

"You will be lucky if you see Stephen Edwards," Dean broke in to say. "He's no match for The Stunning Kid. It looks like to me he left here scared stiff."

"You, Deputy," said The Stunning Kid to Hannibal, "Go get my horse and bring him to the front of the saloon and be quick about it."

Knowing that Thunder was back at the stable, Hannibal ran to the stable, saddled Thunder and rode him to the saloon.

"Your horse is out front," said Hannibal to The Stunning Kid.

"It took you long enough. I was just getting ready to start throwing lead at everybody here, starting with Dean and Ace!" boomed The Stunning Kid.

"Marshal, you and your Deputies pull your guns out and stand watch. Keep Dean and his men here for ten minutes if you know what's good for you. Come on Grubstake, let's get out of here. Don't anybody try and follow us."

The Stunning Kid and Grubstake then left the saloon, climbed on their horses, and rode away.

After they rode a mile out of town, The Stunning Kid suggested to Grubstake that he stay out of sight for a while, until The Dean Dickerson Gang is put behind bars.

"Whatever you do, don't tell anybody I let you go. I don't want The Dean Dickerson Gang to find out," explained The Stunning Kid.

"I thought you were after my gold. Instead your helping me out of a jam," replied a surprised Grubstake to The Stunning Kid. "I won't tell a soul."

Grubstake then continued riding away from Dodge. The Stunning Kid then rode back to Dodge and returned to the saloon as Stephen Edwards.

After ten minutes, The Marshal holstered his gun and informed Dean and his men that they were free to go just as Belle came down the stairs.

"Ace take the men and go after that masked bandit," demanded Dean. "Cover every trail and if you see The Stunning Kid give him the proper reception. Gun him down. If you are able to catch Grubstake, take him to the hideout."

Chapter 21

THE TELEGRAM AND THE WATER HOLE

"Dean, I want you to come up to my office right away," ordered Belle as Ace and the boys left the saloon.

As Belle was back in her office sitting at her desk, she informed Dean that she had been watching from the top of the stairs.

"Stephen Edwards is tough enough. You and the gang should be able to deal with him," reasoned Belle. "It looks like The Stunning Kid is a different story."

"The Stunning Kid keeps showing up when we don't expect him just like what happened downstairs. How did he find out about the prospectors gold so fast?" muttered Dean. "Now it looks like we're going to have to be looking over our shoulder for him.

We have those counterfeit plates that was shipped to you in your hat box. Now we can make all the counterfeit money we want."

"There is a herd of 3,000 head of cattle coming here shortly. The trail boss is going to want water for his cattle. We can charge him a $1.00 a head for water," explained Belle. "I want you and the boys to go and meet that trail boss at our waterhole and collect that money from him. Put a couple of the men on guard to watch for The Stunning Kid. I want to make sure we get that money this time."

There is a gunslinger living in Twin Forks forty miles south of Dodge. Before you go to the water hole, I want you to send a telegram to Michael, The Magnificent in Twin Forks. We have to stop The Stunning Kid from interfering in our plans and I know just the way to do it. Michael doesn't like people. I am going to offer Michael, The Magnificent and his gang $2,000.00 to come to Dodge to do a job for me. Tell Michael to hurry to Dodge.

Take this $1,000.00 and wire it to him in advance. When Michael, The Magnificent and his gang get here, all our worries will be over. I am going to give them the job of going after The Stunning Kid. When he finishes the job, I will pay him another $1,000.00."

"Will you still give me and the boys a crack at it? Do me and the boys get the $2,000.00 if we can catch The Stunning Kid before Michael, The Magnificent and his boys get here?" questioned Dean.

"I really don't think you can catch The Stunning Kid," answered Belle. "The matter has already been decided. Your letting me down. I give you a job to carry out and you and the boys can't get it done. You've been looking high and low for The Stunning Kid. Every time you and the boys had The Stunning Kid in your sights, he outsmarted you. He disappears on you and you don't have any idea where he goes. I suppose you're going to tell me he rides into the sunset and you can't follow him.

If you're lucky enough to catch him, It might do you some good. Then yes, I'll pay you the $2000.00. I can promise you, you won't. I'll believe it when I see it. Now go round up the boys and get going. I don't want any more augments."

After Stephen returned to the saloon, Dean was just coming down from Belle's Office. Marshal Allen, Hannibal, and Scooter was still in the saloon.

"Stephen, where did you go?" asked Hannibal. "You missed out on some excitement. Even though I saw it with my own two optics I thought it was an optical delusion and I didn't believe it. Under the circumflexes, The Marshal, Scooter, and my own self-made Dean and his buddies let the prospector go. They didn't even try to put up a fight. The Stunning Kid was here. We didn't really need him. He only helped a little bit."

"Says who?" replied Stephen.

"Says me," answered Hannibal.

"You Jasper s didn't do anything," objected Dean. "When The Stunning Kid came in with those two Colts, you were shaking in your boots."

"Says who?" Hannibal responded to Dean.

"Says me," challenged Dean. "I want The Stunning Kid and me and my gang are going to get him. I thought I might even catch him myself. If we don't get him, Michael, The Magnificent and his gang are on the way from Twin Forks and they will get him."

"Stop it," ordered The Marshal. "You have nothing to say about it. Stephen, as of now, I am giving you the job to go after The Stunning Kid. If anybody can find him, you can. Nobody is exempt from the law."

"Stephen is going after The Stunning Kid," laughed Dean. "The only thing he can catch is a cold."

"Come on Stephen. Let's go back to the office and start planning how your going to catch The Stunning Kid," requested The Marshal.

Chapter 22

THE PLANNING OF THE TELEGRAM AND THE WATER HOLE

Thirty minutes later Ace and the boys returned to the saloon and followed Dean into his office. Seeing the gang returning to town, Stephen quickly left The Marshal's Office and went around behind Belle's Saloon and climbed on the roof over Dean's Office to listen in to Dean and the gang.

"I guess we lost The Stunning Kid. It's hard to keep up with him. We tried to trail him, but he gave us the slip," Ace said to Dean. "He's always on the move and just disappears into thin air. The Stunning Kid seems to know every move we make before we do it. He's always one up on us."

"Stop yelping like a coyote," ordered Dean. "We need to take care of The Kid by putting one over on him. If we can capture that stupid Deputy, Scooter, we can use him as bait. The Stunning Kid will follow us to try and get him back.

When he follows us, everything will be all set. We'll have The Stunning Kid where we want him. He'll be riding into a trap. He will have a lot of worries on his mind, because he is going to know he's in a bind. That will be more than he can handle. For him it will be all or nothing.

Belle wants me to send a telegram to Michael, The Magnificent who lives in Twin Forks. If we don't get The Stunning Kid, Michael and his gang will be paid $2,000.00 to get rid of The Stunning Kid. If we can get him before Michael gets here, we can divide the $2,000.00. That should make Belle happy.

Belle wants us to send the telegram on our way out of town to the water hole to help Rusty and Henry, who is camped out there. A trail boss is coming with a herd 3,000 cattle. He is going to have to water his cattle and he will need water now. He will be forced to give us a $1.00 for every steer that gets watered. It's a two day ride to the next water hole and his cattle won't make it. They will be dropping like flies.

OK you guys. We have business to attend to. After we collect the $3,000.00 from the trail boss, we need to get busy and find Scooter."

"I got news for you about Scooter," insisted Ace.

"What's all this about Scooter?" ranted Dean.

"Scooter may not be as dumb as you think. I found out that Stephen and Hannibal work for Scooter and he is smarter than he seems," explained Ace. "When Scooter starts to shiver all over, nobody knows what he is going to do. The people who know him run and hide because he can be a killer. When I find him, I would like to shove that tin star down his throat,"

"That's what you think. What put that notice in your head?" answered Dean. "You keep that Deputy healthy. I don't want to have to say things twice. Remember, he's our bait to catch The Stunning Kid.

He's too stupid to be anybody's boss."

"Yes, I know," answered Ace. "But I thought."

"That's ridiculous. You thought what? Where did you get that idea?" boomed Dean.

"I can't tell you. You wouldn't believe me if I did," replied Ace.

"Is Ace, The Assassin afraid of Scooter? You better not be!" yelled Dean.

"Don't worry boss. I'm not afraid of that nuisance," insisted Ace.

"Come on. Snap it up. All of you. You better be getting to your horses and now. We got to get to the water hole before the trail boss gets there with his cattle. It's not going to take care of itself. If we can find Scooter today, then maybe we can get rid of The Stunning Kid.

Tomorrow, the owner of The Golden Moon Mine is sending out a large shipment of gold on the stage. I want The Stunning Kid out of the way so we can get that gold. If Lucky Lewis loses the gold shipment, he won't be able to pay me for the machinery he bought from me. Then he will have to give me his gold mine. That ought to make Belle happy."

"How much gold are they shipping?" asked Lefty.

"There is only one way to find out. Hold up the stage," answered Dean. "Let's get rolling."

Chapter 23

STEPHEN REPORTS TO THE MARSHAL

And Now It's Just The Three OF Us

Stephen immediately climbed off the roof of the saloon and headed to The Marshal's Office.

"Marshal, I just overheard Dean making plans with his bunch of cutthroats to capture Scooter and use him as bait for The Stunning Kid," Stephen went on to say. "It also turns out that Belle is the leader of The Dean Dickerson Gang. She told Dean to telegraph Michael, The Magnificent, who lives in Twin Forks to hire him to come and kill The Stunning Kid."

"That was very destructive to my curiosity," broke in Hannibal.

"It looks like we're going to have to keep a constant eye on Scooter," insisted The Marshal.

"No, I have a better idea. Rex, if you or Don is listening," asked Stephen. "Get Scooter home as soon as possible. It looks like we're going to need more help right away. I need you to send us three handheld two way radios now. Would you get the rest of The West Side Kids ready to come and help us?"

"I want to stay here and help you," said Scooter. And then he disappeared.

"I don't know what to say. That was a sight to see," said the surprised Marshal. "I've seen a lot of things in my life. I've never seen anything like that before."

"Now there is just the three of us," reasoned Stephen as the three radios appeared on The Marshal's desk. "We have to get out of our own troubles. Hannibal, you stay with The Marshal at all times for the safety of both of you.

Our next problem is at Dean Dickerson's water hole. A herd of 3,000 cattle is coming up from the south to get water. Dean Dickerson and his gang are on their way to the water hole right now. The trail boss is going to be charged a $1.00 for every steer that is watered. You and Hannibal need to find the trail boss right away to help him get water for his herd without paying Mr. Dickerson.

Marshal, before you go, I need you to draw me a map of the area. Then I am going to give each of you a two way radio. Marshal, Hannibal will show you how to use it. As The Stunning Kid I will need to know the lay of the land when I get to the water hole. I want The Dickerson Gang to chase me and when they do, I will call you on the two way radio to get those cattle to the water hole right away."

Just as Stephen was going to tell The Marshal about the gold shipment the door to The Marshal's Office opened. Lucky Lewis, owner of The Golden Moon Mine, came through the door.

"Hello Marshal. I'm here to tell you that I'm going to ship a strong box full of gold from my mine tomorrow," Lucky announced to The Marshal. "Would you and your Deputies escort the stage with my gold tomorrow. I owe Dean Dickerson for the machinery I bought from him to use in my mine. I need the gold and I can't afford to lose it. If I can't pay Dean Dickerson, he will foreclose and get the mine."

"If you tell me what time the stage is leaving tomorrow," answered The Marshal. "Me and my Deputies will be there."

"The stage is leaving nice and early tomorrow at 7:00 a. m.," answered Lucky.

"We'll see you tomorrow," answered The Marshal.

After Lucky left Stephen said to The Marshal, "The gold shipment was the other thing I overheard Dean tell his men. They are planning to rob the stage. That's what they think. I'm not going with you as a guard tomorrow. I think its better that The Stunning Kid watch the stage from a distance."

Chapter 24

SCOOTER RETURNS TO THE 21ST CENTURY

Traveling through time to the present, Scooter is now in Rex's Office.

"Hi Scooter." greeted Rex. "Why did Stephen want me to bring you back to the present time? Are you guys making any progress back in Dodge?"

"Howdy partner," answered Scooter. "It would go faster if Marshal Dillon were there to help us. Dean Dickerson and his gang was going to try and kidnap me. That's why I'm back here. Am I here to stay?"

"No, you're going back. Now that we know we can go back and forth in time, Columbo, The West Side Kids and I are going with you. Tell me everything that's happened, so we can go back with a plan. You didn't try to blow up Dean Dickerson's Saloon and that's why they are after you?" asked Rex.

"No, I didn't try to blow up Dean's Saloon. Very funny. I forgot to laugh," boomed Scooter. "Stephen said Dean Dickerson wants to use me as bait to catch The Stunning Kid."

"You must know that when Ace took your coin and disappeared, he appeared in my office," explained Rex. "Columbo and I was able to find out a lot from Ace about what was going on in Dodge. Now we're all going to help. At this moment, Columbo is instructing the boys on firearms, police techniques and horseback riding.

I told Ace that you was Stephen and Hannibal's boss. That you was very tough and even a killer. When you start to shiver, everybody better take cover because of what you might do.

Columbo, the gang and me are going back in time with you. I want to start from outside Dodge City. When we go back, you will be a U. S. Marshal and the rest of us will be your Deputies with you riding in front."

"Am I going to be like Roy Rogers?" questioned Scooter. "If I'm going to be like Roy Rogers, then Hannibal will have to be Gabby Hayes."

"Your darn toot-in. Hannibal will be Gabby Hayes," agreed Rex.

Chapter 25

THE STUNNING KID RIDES AGAIN

As Scooter and Rex talked, The Marshal sat at his desk back in Dodge City making a map for Stephen and when he finished Stephen said, "It's time for The Stunning Kid to ride again."

"Are you serious? You're taking this Stunning Kid character too seriously." laughed Hannibal. "I reckon you're watching too many John Wayne movies, partner. Your getting to sound like The Lone Ranger, so I must be Tonto. Show The Marshal your silver bullets, then take Silver and get moving Pilgrim. Can I ride Lightning on this venture?"

"Go ahead and take him," answered Stephen. "He can use the exercise. If you ride my white horse, you can't be John Wayne or even Roy Rogers. You'll have to settle for being The Lone Ranger who is riding Silver."

"Very funny," replied Hannibal. "What are you doing, filling in for Scooter while he's gone?"

"All right boys stop it!" screamed The Marshal. "Instead of fighting with each other, we need to work together."

"Oh, we're not really fighting Marshal," explained Hannibal. "We're just having fun giving each other a hard time. Right now, Scooter is safe and Stephen is going in harm's way. I just want Stephen to be careful. He's not Scooter, and I don't want him to do anything stupid with The Dean Dickerson Gang. Stephen is my friend and I want him to come back safe.

There is no one who can replace Stephen. There are too many people at home who need and depend upon him. Besides, I don't want you to get stuck fighting The Dean Dickerson Gang with just you, Marshal. I not good enough to help you like Stephen. I don't want anything to happen to him by doing something stupid. Do you understand me?"

"OK Chief, I won't do anything stupid. I'll be careful," answered Stephen. "You and The Marshal stay safe and don't you do anything stupid."

"It sounds like we both miss Scooter by the way were talking. Doesn't that scare you a little bit?" reasoned Hannibal. "At least Scooter is safe."

"Ya, I think I miss him to. There's nobody like Scooter. He does rub off on you. It looks like we'll have to finish this job without him," replied Stephen.

"He is very different," added The Marshal. "You can't help but like him."

"When we get back from the water hole, we can talk about the gold shipment and Michael, The Magnificent and his gang coming to Dodge. I don't want Michael, The Magnificent to make the trip to Dodge for nothing. Come on. Let's Head Em Up and Move Em Out."

"Stephen, your sounding like a trail boss. Just who is this John Wayne character you keep talking about?" asked The Marshal. "Now you're talking about The Lone Ranger, Tonto and silver bullets. Why would anyone use silver bullets? Why spend all that money on silver bullets? Just using the normal kind of bullets are expensive enough. I never noticed. Does Stephen use silver bullets as The Stunning Kid?"

"No, Stephen doesn't use silver bullets. It's a long story. I'll tell you on the way to the water hole," replied Hannibal. "Then when we come back, we'll tell you about Chuck Norris and Clint Eastwood. As long as were at it, we'll even tell you about Superman."

"Superman. Just who is Superman?" asked The Marshal.

"Just hold that thought," replied Hannibal. "Let's just wait until we all get back so our friend the masked man, disguised as Stephen Edwards can help explain who all these people are."

Thirty minutes later as The Stunning Kid was approaching the water hole and The Dean Dickerson Gang, he pulled out his two way radio from his saddle bags.

"Marshal, Hannibal, can you hear me?" asked The Stunning Kid. "Over."

"I can hear you," answered Hannibal. "The Marshal is trying to figure out how his two way radio works, over."

"I can hear you," replied The Marshal. "I can't believe I can hear you on this thing you gave me. I guess now I'm supposed to say over."

"You can believe it and your learning," insisted The Stunning Kid. "I'm at the water hole and so is Dean Dickerson, over."

"We're about ten minutes from the water hole," said The Marshal. "And I can see the trail boss, over."

"When you get to the water hole, I'm going to come in shooting," explained The Stunning Kid. "When The Dean Dickerson gang starts chasing me, get those cattle watered right away, over."

"It's as good as done," insisted Hannibal. "Over and out."

Ten minutes later, the herd reached the water hole. As Dean Dickerson climbed on his horse to ride up to the trail boss, The Stunning Kid began to ride toward the water hole on Thunder, with both guns blazing away. As The Dean Dickerson Gang began to fire back, The Stunning Kid turned Thunder around and rode away as The Dean Dickerson Gang chased him.

Down the dirt road The Stunning Kid went with Thunder at a full gallop. Right behind him followed The Dickerson Gang, firing their guns at will. Through the trees and around the bushes rode The Stunning Kid as he approached the hills decorated with large boulders.

Up the hill he went leading The Dickerson Gang away from the water hole. After The Stunning Kid reached the top of the hill, he rode behind two large boulders, out of sight of The Dickerson Gang. After The Dickerson Gang rode past him, The Stunning Kid rode back around the boulders shooting his guns in the air. The Dickerson Gang turned their horses around and continued the chase.

Down the hill The Stunning Kid rode Thunder. Down the hill followed The Dickerson Gang, aiming their guns and firing at The Stunning Kid. The Stunning Kid was far enough ahead of The Dickerson Gang where he was able to ride Thunder behind some very tall bushes, undetected from The Dickerson Gang.

He threw the loop of his rope over a big tall bush, winding the other end of the rope around his saddle horn and backed Thunder in behind some trees. There the rope lay on the ground from the bush to the saddle horn. As the gang rode up to the rope, The Stunning Kid backed Thunder up pulling the rope off the ground where it was tight and high enough to knock the gang off their horses as they rode under it. He then rode Thunder up to the gang with both guns drawn.

"You know the drill," laughed The Stunning Kid. "Throw your guns on the ground and then take your boots off and throw them in the bushes. Now you can start walking back to town."

"It's bad enough that you're making us walk back to town," reasoned Dean. "At least let us keep our boots."

"I said take off your boots and throw them in the bushes," answered The Stunning Kid as he shot a couple of warning shots in the ground. "While your at it, take off your pants and throw them in the bushes and be quick about it."

After the gang took off their pants and boots with their long underwear showing they threw their boots and pants into the bushes, The Stunning Kid then fired a couple of warning shots in the ground scaring the horses. The gang then turned and ran as their horses bolted out of sight.

After the gang was out of sight, The Stunning Kid called The Marshal on his two way radio and asked about the heard getting water. The Marshal reported that everything was going as planned. The Stunning Kid then rode back around the bushes circling back to town.

Not knowing where The Stunning Kid was, Dean stopped his gang to talk to them and said, "With Rusty and Henry, that makes us eight. We had the numbers and The Stunning Kid made fools out of all of us. I want that Stunning Kid and I want him now! It's bad enough we have to walk back to town, but when he took our pants and boots, ouch, ouch, ouch. I'll get him for this, ouch, ouch, ouch. This is embarrassing. OK, let's get back to town to get fresh horses and some pants and boots!"

After The Dean Dickerson Gang walked back to Dodge, they limped their way to Belle's Saloon as people gawked at them, laughing at the gang. Wanting to find Scooter to complete the next part of their plan by going down every street, searching every building to find Scooter was out of the question. Realizing they had been a failure at the water hole by not able to catch The Stunning Kid or not wanting to find Scooter, Dean reluctantly went to Belle's Office.

As Dean went through the office door, he saw Belle sitting at her desk.

"Show me the money," requested Belle with a smile on her face.

"What money?' muttered Dean with a scared look in his eyes.

"The $3,000.00 you took from the trail boss," stormed Belle. "You did get the money?"

"No, I didn't get the money," muttered Dean as he was looking straight down at Belle's desk.

"That was an easy job I gave you and the boys," boomed Belle. "How could anything go wrong? You look awful. Where's your pants and your boots?"

"What do you mean easy job. I don't know how, but The Stunning Kid found out about the trail herd and the water hole. There was no way he could find out, but he did. He came riding towards us with both guns blazing. We returned fire and chased him," Dean went on to say. "He ambushed us and took all of our pants and boots. It was a long embarrassing walk back to town with no pants and boots and my feet really hurt. I'm going to get him for that.

We lost him, the $3,000.00 our pants and our boots. Since we had to walk back to town with no boots, the trail boss watered his herd and we didn't get the $3,000"

"You was just a tin horn from Chicago when I found you. I pay you big money to be the boss of my gang. Scooter could probably run this gang better than you," insisted Belle. "Even though he is always doing something stupid, I'm sure he would have come back with the $3,000.00 or The Stunning Kid, maybe both.

Tomorrow is the shipment of gold from The Golden Moon Mine. Do you think you can get that gold off the stage or do I need to go along and hold your hand?"

"We were doing fine until The Stunning Kid came to our territory!" shouted Dean. "You just come along and find out how easy it is after The Stunning Kid comes shooting straight at you. It doesn't make any difference how much you are paying me if a slug from one of his guns finishes me off."

"You just get that shipment of gold off of the stage tomorrow or I'll have to make a deal with Michael, The Magnificent to take over," promised Belle.

"You do that any time you want," replied Dean. "Things are just getting too hot around here for me."

Chapter 26

THE GOLD SHIPMENT

It is now 7 a. m., the next morning and the stage is leaving Dodge. The Marshal is riding next to the driver with a loaded shot gun. Hannibal is sitting behind The Marshal and the driver with a loaded Winchester rifle.

"I never thought I would ever be riding on a stage with a Winchester," remarked Hannibal. "This is just like in the movie, Stagecoach with John Wayne on top of the stage with a Winchester. All we need now is for the Indians to attack while I sit here and shoot at them. Next we need The cavalry to come and rescue us."

"What are you talking about?" asked the driver. "There are no Indians around here. The cavalry is miles away from here."

"Don't pay any attention to what he's saying and just drive," ordered The Marshal. "You wouldn't understand in a million years."

As the stage rolled on, The Stunning Kid followed the stage along the ridge of the hill.

A couple miles down the road was The Dean Dickerson Gang. As the stage approached them, Ace said to Danny, "Go lie down in the road. When the driver sees you, he will stop."

Danny got off of his horse and walked over to the middle of the road and laid down. As the stage approached Danny, the driver stopped the coach.

Danny stood up with his face covered with a mask and yelled with his gun drawn, "This is a hold up. Drop your guns and reach for the sky."

"Do as he says," said The Marshal to Hannibal.

"You don't have to tell me twice. This isn't the way it happened in the movie with John Wayne. I would rather fight the Indians and have the cavalry rescue us," answered Hannibal.

"What's this about John Wayne, The cavalry and Indians?" asked Danny

"I don't know," explained the driver. "That's the second time he said that about John Wayne, the cavalry and the Indians since he climbed on top of the stage."

Ace, Lefty, Mugs and Shorty then rode to the stage, with their faces covered and guns drawn, surrounding the stage.

"What's with this John Wayne, the cavalry and the Indians?" shouted Ace.

"You'll never understand in a million years," explained The Marshal.

"Then let's get on with this hold up. Throw down that strong box," ordered Ace.

Just as Ace started to climb down from his horse, The Stunning Kid rode his horse Thunder at a fast pace towards the stage and The Dickerson Gang with his colt drawn, he began firing.

"It's The Stunning Kid again," yelled Ace. "Can't we do at least one job without that masked varmint interfering? Come on boys, let's give him a reception he'll never forget."

"Not me!" screamed Lefty. "I tangled with him once to often and I don't want to do it again. Let's make a run for it!"

"Dean isn't going to like us running from The Stunning Kid," screamed Ace with his gun drawn as The Stunning Kid shot it out of his hand.

"The rest of you stay and shoot it out with The Stunning Kid!" Ace screamed again. "If Dean wants The Stunning Kid and the $2,000.00, he's welcome to both! I'm getting out of here!"

"Everybody get out of the way!" yelled Lefty. "I'm out of here!"

The Dickerson Gang then turned their horses away from The Stunning Kid and began to ride away with The Stunning Kid chasing them with his guns blazing away.

"Well Marshal, he's no John Wayne," Hannibal went on to say. "He will do. The Stunning Kid saved the day."

"Why do you keep talking about this John Wayne character?" asked the stage driver. "Marshal, if he's so great, it just makes sense to hire him as your Deputy. I think he would help you more than this great Stephen Edwards. He is never around to help you when you need him."

"You will never know how much help Stephen Edwards is," explained The Marshal. "I gave Stephen Edwards the job to find The Stunning Kid. If anybody can find him, Stephen can. I'm sure The Stunning Kid knows about Stephen looking for him. Whenever Stephen shows up somewhere, The Stunning Kid disappears. Stephen is doing a fine job. John Wayne is not available for hire."

A couple minutes into the chase, The Dickerson Gang approaches a herd of cattle along the road.

"There's a herd of cattle beside the road," exclaimed Ace. "Let's stampede the cattle and turn them back on The Stunning Kid. That will be the end of him and then we can get back to pulling jobs without The Stunning Kid interfering all of the time."

The Dickerson gang then got behind the cattle, shooting their guns in the air, stampeding the cattle towards The Stunning Kid. The Stunning Kid turned Thunder around and rode toward a hill full of large boulders away from the cattle.

When The Stunning Kid reached the top of the hill away from the cattle, he said, "Thunder, they are up one on us this time. At least we saved the stage from being robbed. Let's get back to town."

Seeing The Stunning Kid ride up the hills through the large boulders, Ace said to the gang, "The Stunning Kid is getting away, after him."

Having a head start, The Stunning Kid rode around a large boulder next to the road. He dismounted off of Thunder and climbed on top of the boulder and crouched down facing the road. Ace and Lefty rode past the boulder followed by Shorty and Mugs. Last was

Danny. As Danny passed the boulder, The Stunning Kid jumped off the boulder on Danny knocking him off of his horse and on to the ground. Both men immediately stood up and The Stunning Kid gave Danny a right to the jaw, knocking him out.

"Danny's gone," yelled Mugs. "The Stunning Kid got him. There's The Kid's horse."

"Get off your horses and find The Kid. He's got to be around here somewhere," ordered Ace.

The gang with guns drawn, began to look on foot for The Stunning Kid. Lefty decided to walk between two large boulders in his search. After reaching the other side of the boulders, a left arm swung around knocking Lefty out.

"One, two, three, four, five, that's enough, he's out. I win," said The Stunning Kid to himself.

The Stunning Kid then disappeared around two other boulders and waited as Ace, Mugs and Shorty appeared.

With both guns drawn, The Stunning Kid looked down at the boots of Ace, Mugs and Shorty. He then began to look up slowly to their faces and then yelled BOO, scaring the trio so bad that they turned around and started running.

The Stunning Kid then started to laugh as he was yelling, "This is the fourth or fifth time I've tangled with you buzzards. Who remembers? If I ever catch you trying to rob another stage or if you intimidate any more homesteaders, you won't get off so easy. Now you collect the other two rats of your gang and ride."

Chapter 27

MICHAEL, THE MAGNIFICENT

As the gang rode away, The Stunning Kid began ridding back to town on a dirt road past some bushes and he heard a moan.

"Whoa Thunder," commanded The Stunning Kid. "I thought I heard somebody moaning like they are really in pain."

The Stunning Kid then rode around the bushes looking for the injured person who was making the sound of pain. Seconds later he rode up to a person laying on the ground.

"Are you OK? Do you need some help?" asked The Stunning Kid.

"I'm afraid you got me. My right leg is broken, and I can't defend myself," cried the man laying on the ground. Pulling the money out of his pocket and presenting it to The Stunning Kid, the man said, "Here take my money if you're going to rob me. Would you at least help me back on my horse?"

"Oh, the mask. That's why you think I'm going to rob you. Now if I only had some silver bullets. I don't want your money. I'm not going to rob you," replied The Stunning Kid. "If you let me, I can reset your leg and then I will make camp so you can rest."

"I can really use your help. If you hadn't found me, I would have died," reasoned the man. "My name is Michael, The Magnificent. Who are you and why the mask? What did you say about silver bullets?"

"Oh, the silver bullets. It was nothing. I don't even know why I said that," answered The Stunning Kid. "I am an outlaw known as The Stunning Kid. That's why the mask.

Don't worry about me. I am going to see that you are well taken care of. I thought I saw a doctor back down the road away. Let me get you comfortable and then I will go find him."

The Stunning Kid then walked over to Michael, The Magnificence's horse and took the saddle and blanket off. He then walked over to Michael and laid the blanket on the ground and then placed the saddle as a pillow for Michael to lay on.

"I'll be back in a few minutes after I get the doctor. You have your gun for protection, and you should be alright until I get back," said The Stunning Kid.

The Stunning Kid then got on Thunder and rode away out of Michael's sight.

"Rex, Rex can you hear me?" asked The Stunning Kid. "I need you to find me a doctor right away, to come and reset a broken leg of Michael, The Magnificent. I need to help so I can make friends with him right away. I realize it's a short notice, but I can't leave him alone on the road to die. He doesn't know it yet. Belle is going to hire him to kill me."

A minute later, an envelope with a note inside appeared on the road in front of The Stunning Kid. He climbed down from Thunder and picked up the envelope and pulled out the note that read, "A doctor will be there shortly. Go back to Michael and wait."

The Stunning Kid then climbed back on Thunder and rode back to Michael.

"I didn't really think you would be back," said an anxious Michael. "The pain in my right leg is getting to be unbearable."

"I told you I would be back. The doctor will be here in a little while," promised The Stunning Kid. "Let me round up some wood for a campfire. Then I'll make some coffee. The doctor should be here by then."

As the water in the coffee pot started to heat up to be used with instant coffee, the doctor was seen walking toward them with a doctor's bag.

"Hello boys. I'm Doctor Genesis. I assume that's the patient laying on the blanket."

"Hello doctor. Am I glad to see you," said an anxious Michael. "My name is Michael, The Magnificent, an outlaw. I don't know why, and I can't believe the two of you are helping me. I am very indebted to both of you and I want to thank you for your help. I owe both of you for saving my life.

That somehow bothers me. Some people are just plain warm and friendly. I'm not a warm and friendly person. That's why I stay away from warm and friendly people. They seem to take advantage of me every time. That's not my idea of friendship. If I had found somebody like me along the road, I would have left them to die."

"You don't owe us anything," replied The Stunning Kid. "We don't help people just because they are warm and friendly. Our reward is helping anybody in time of need. If in the future you need my help again, I will be there for you as long as I am not breaking the law to help you."

The doctor then proceeded in taking Michael's temperature, getting his blood pressure and everything a 21st century doctor would do before he began to reset Michael's leg. After the doctor finished with Michael's right leg, he gave Michael a bottle of pills, crutches and a letter explaining how to take care of his broken leg.

"Thanks doc. What do I owe you?" asked Michael.

"You don't owe me a thing. I was glad I was able to help," replied Doctor Genesis. The doctor then picked up his bag and walked back down the road in the direction he came and disappeared as The Stunning Kid and Michael sat by the campfire drinking coffee and talking.

After a half hour passed, The Stunning Kid said to Michael, "If your ready, let me ride into Dodge with you. I can't go all the way in. You should be able to make it the rest of the way on your own."

"A snake scared my horse and bucked me off," explained Michael. "I was on my way to Dodge to Belle's Saloon to find Belle. She hired me to do a job for $2,000.00. I don't know what the job is. It doesn't make any difference now because I can't do it anyway. The rest of my gang is coming to Dodge. I was in line to do the job. My gang will have to do it for me."

Fifteen minutes later, Michael and The Stunning Kid was at the edge of Dodge City.

"I'm going to have to let you ride in alone to Dodge from here. Belle's Saloon is right across from The Marshal's Office," said The Stunning Kid. "There is a tough, nosy Deputy Marshal by the name of Stephen Edwards who would like to see me in his jail. If you run into him, don't tell him what you're doing in Dodge. He may be just as happy to put you in his jail."

"Thanks for the tip my friend and for saving my life. If for any reason you are in a jam and need help of any kind, I will be there to help you," promised Michael.

"I better go now. Take care of yourself," urged The Stunning Kid. "Come on Thunder. Let's get out of here."

Chapter 28

Two Ends Against The Middle

Five minutes later, Michael, The Magnificent rode up to Belle's Saloon just as Ace and the gang was in front of the saloon getting off of their horses.

"Are you boys going into the saloon?" asked Michael.

"What of it?" ranted Ace. "Is there something we can do for you?"

"You wouldn't happen to know Belle? She sent for me," explained Michael. "I have a broken right leg. Would you help me get off my horse?"

"You wouldn't happen to be Michael, The Magnificent?" asked Ace.

"Yes I am. How do you know that?" questioned Michael just as Deputy Marshal Stephen Edwards walked up to Michael.

"Who have we got here, Ace?" demanded Stephen. "Another member of your gang?"

"What of it?" roared Ace. "He hasn't broken any laws."

"I don't know what you do," inquired Stephen as he was looking at Michael. "I'm here to enforce the laws of Dodge City, so watch your step."

"Well Mr. lawman. If my leg wasn't broken, you wouldn't be talking to me like that," snapped Michael. "My boys are on their way to Dodge. When they get here you better watch your step or else, they may get very angry with you."

"Lefty and Danny, help Michael off of his horse. Shorty go get Belle and tell her that Michael, The Magnificent is here," ordered Ace.

"What kind of name is Michael, The Magnificent," asked Stephen. "That's one thing I can't stand is people with funny names like that. Another hombre that is somewhere in The Dodge City area with a funny name like that calls himself The Stunning Kid. One of these days he is going to find himself in The Marshal's Office if I have anything to do with it."

"You better not even think about going after him, Mr. Deputy Marshal," ordered Michael. "He found me with a broken leg along the road outside Dodge where my horse bucked me off. He saved my life. The Stunning Kid is a fine person. You try going after him and it will have to be between you and me. I will be forced to shoot you down."

"I can hardly wait to see the look on Belle's face when she hears about this," laughed Ace. "Michael, you're not going to like what we have to report to Belle. Come on Michael. Let's go find Belle."

"Don't walk too fast," ordered Michael. "I'm not very fast with these crutches."

"Then we better go to my office in the back of the saloon," offered Dean who was listening at the front door to the saloon. "Belle's Office is on the second floor and it would be very difficult for you to go up those stairs."

Hearing Dean invite Michael to his office, Stephen disappeared around to the back of the saloon and climbed on the roof over Dean's office to listen to the meeting.

A couple of minutes later, Dean was inviting Michael, The Magnificent in his office.

"Welcome, come on in Michael. It's a great honor to have you here. I'm glad you could make it. Sit down. Sit down. Have a seat," offered Dean as Belle, Dean, Ace and the entire gang followed Michael into Dean's Office. As Michael sat down, Belle then sat down next to Michael in front of Dean's desk.

"How do you do Michael. So, your Michael, The Magnificent. What happened to your right leg?" asked Belle.

"That's the reason I'm late getting here. I have never been late for anything before. A couple of miles out of town, a snake scared my horse and bucked me off," explained Michael. "An outlaw by the name of The Stunning Kid found me and saved my life. He even found a doctor who was dressed like a tenderfoot to reset my leg. Although he did a good job resetting my leg, he had some strange tools in his doctor's bag that I never seen before. After he reset my leg, he put this cast on it.

I don't like people and I never would have done that for anybody, especially a stranger. I would have rode away and let him die. If The Stunning Kid had thought like that, who knows what would have happen to me. Since The Stunning Kid helped me, I owe him my life and I always pay my debts."

"I just don't know what to say," said a surprised Belle. "I wired you a $1,000.00 in advance to do a job for me and you accepted. Now your not going to like the job I hired you to do. We can't pull off any jobs since The Stunning Kid came to this territory. Your job is to go after The Stunning Kid and finish him off."

"I can't do that. I'll have to pass," cried Michael. "He saved my life and I owe him. You mean to say that the debt I owe The Stunning Kid, I will never be able to repay?"

"Don't get riled up. I won't take no for an answer and I'm going to be forced to say if you refuse to do the job that we made a deal on, I'm holding you to it. That's how it works. As you say, you always pay your debts," demanded Belle. "You don't understand. He's our number one problem. He is ruining our gang."

"You tell him Belle," beamed Dean. "Michael, it looks to me like you've got a problem. You are indebted to two people. Guess who's going to get it. If you pay one of your debts, you can't pay the other one. If you don't go after The Stunning Kid, Belle will be coming after you. This I've got to see. If I were you, I would hop along right out of this territory and don't come back."

"Let's talk this over. I can explain everything that's happened. Everything will be explained to your satisfaction. I'm in this fix because I don't like people. Because of what The Stunning Kid did for me, I can't help but like him," explained Michael. "I can't do this because of my broken leg. When my gang shows up here in Dodge, they will have to do the job for me."

"How many men do you have in your gang?" asked Belle.

"There are five men who are on their way to Dodge. They'll be coming tomorrow to join up with me," answered Michael. "There is Tiny, Art, Big Bob, Charlie, The Chill and The Oklahoma Kid."

"Hopefully, that will be enough," replied Belle.

"It will be more than enough," reasoned Michael. "I really wish there was seven of us all together. Then we would be The Magnificent Seven."

"I don't care how many of you are in your gang. Just see that they get the job done," instructed Belle. "Your men are going to have their hands full of The Stunning Kid when they start looking for him. He goes after all those badmen working for me by himself and doesn't need any help. He rides like the wind.

We don't know where he disappears to except, he always rides into the sunset. The best way to find him is to have a plan to get him to come looking for you. He is full of tricks and fast with his guns. When are your men going to be here?"

"They should be here by tomorrow afternoon," replied Michael.

"Ace, your next. How did things go? Even no news is good news. You have a gift for me? Where is the money? Tell me, did you get the gold from The Golden Moon Mine off the stage this time?" questioned Belle. "I didn't see you carry it in. Did you and the boys leave the gold in your saddle bags?"

"Well it's like this Belle," Ace began to say. "We was in the process of having stopped the stage and guess who showed up with both guns blazing?"

"Oh, oh, I know what your going to say. Don't think you can fool me. You didn't get the gold? They say that money is the root of all evil. Wealth is even a curse to me because I don't have it," cried Belle. "I know somebody that is rich millionaires. They have so much money that they can even afford to have separate salt and pepper shakers.

With Rusty and Henry, there was seven of you and you let one person stop you. What kind of men do I have working for me? Is The Stunning Kid too much for you? It sounds like the whole thing has been a bust. You had your chance to catch The Stunning Kid and get paid the $2,000.00 and instead you ran. At least you came back with your pants and boots."

"Your right Belle. I have a good reason for that. The boys and I are taking all the risks. I was going to give him the proper reception we planned on," explained Ace. "I know how to shoot and had my gun drawn and aimed at The Kid. The next thing I knew he was riding up to us in his glory. He has flaming guns that shoot all day long without reloading and he shot my gun out of my hand.

That rascal can really shoot. I heard a rumor that he has killed seven people with one bullet. That's The Stunning Kid alright.

Believe me Belle, I was going to stand my ground and fight. When I saw my gun laying on the ground it was too dangerous to stay. There was only one thing left to do. Forget the gold and make a run for it."

"Where did you hide from that rascal?" asked Belle.

"After he chased us down the road, yonder we saw a herd of cattle. We rode around the herd and fired our guns in the air to stampede the cattle towards The Stunning Kid," Ace continued to say. "We thought that was going to finish him He never makes a wrong move, because he rode away on The Sunset Trail and got away."

"He didn't get away on The Sunset Trail," laughed Michael. "His escape as you call it, happened to be on the road where my horse bucked me off and he found me. If he hadn't come down what you call The Sunset Trail, that could have been my last sunset. It sounds to me that you're just making an excuse to Belle as to why you didn't chase him."

"This is terrible. This is very terrible. Well Michael, now you see why I sent for you," laughed Belle. "Ace and the boys are not definitely a credit to their profession. They aren't doing anything to stop The Stunning Kid. The job is getting too tough for my little angels and they come back crying to mama."

"Belle, that's uncalled for! You're out of your mind. You seem to think money grows on trees!" yelled Ace. "I don't see you out there helping with these jobs. If you were there, you would be the first to run after The Stunning Kid's bullets blazed past your ears. I'm sure you're going to tell us that you would fire your gun and finish off The Stunning Kid for good."

"You see what I have to put up with Michael," replied Belle. "We had a good operation going on here until The Stunning Kid showed up. That's too bad. We were doing so well.

That's pitiful, very pitiful. I thought I hired men. That was my mistake. When I keep hearing Dean say that he will get the boys to do the job, he really means it. These are not men working for me. They are overgrown worthless boys.

That's where you come in. I hope I'm not making the same mistake with you. I saw a chance to hook up with you and hired you from your reputation as Michael, The Magnificent. I did hire real men this time, didn't I? It's going to take real men to go after The Stunning Kid.

I never meant The Stunning Kid. He's getting to be a legend in his own time. I wish I could get him to work for me because that's a real man. I would love to make a fuss over him and get him to take off his mask so I can see how cute he is. What was he like?"

"He is a real man and a good friend. You have to admire him for that," explained Michael. "If you meant him, you would really like him. He's a rip snorting shooting-est crack shot and a blue tail marvel. He doesn't have to put on Aires to prove he's a fighting, biggest, hardest, strongest, roughest, bravest man alive."

"I have tangled with him before and I have never seen anybody with a left hook like his before," broke in Ace.

"That's right, you should know," replied Dean. "You tangled with Deputy Marshal Stephen Edwards and didn't see anything for a while."

"There ain't no girl good enough for The Stunning Kid. Some heroes are fighters. Some heroes are lovers," Belle continued to say. "In fact, there are rumors going around that he only loves his horse and someday they will be buried together."

"After he saved my life, I felt like I was in his debt and told him so. It just doesn't set right with me that my men have to go after him and finish him off. Especially a man like him," reasoned Michael.

"This is ridicules. This is impossible. It can't be done. I have been doing some high powered thinking. I found out a long time ago that if you define the problem correctly, you almost have the solution and that's what I did to come up with a couple of ideas.

Although I'm not officially in the gang yet, I have developed a plan where I can finish the job you hired me to do. I'm tempted to do this if it will get me out of this jam, I will do the best I can to get out of this jam if you let me work on my plan with no strings attached.

It's just plain insanity, but it might work. The ole brain gets rusty if you don't use it. Not neither me nor my gang will have to try and track The Stunning Kid down or even finish him off."

"You're kidding. Nothing gets by that ole fox," replied Belle. "That won't bother me none if there are no strings attached. I have to admire your pride in coming up with the plans you are going to use to take care of our problem."

"There is one thing left and then we can wrap things up. Belle, do you have a cabin where your boys and my men can meet and work on my ideas?" asked Michael.

"Michael, I don't like that crack about your men and Belle's boys," objected Ace. "No more. I ought to let you have it."

"Calm down Ace!" screamed Belle. "We need to be working together and not against each other. You boys had your chance to get The Stunning Kid. Now let's wait until Michael's men get here and then listen to what he has to say. Now Ace, are you going to let me have it because of what I said?"

"No Belle, I'm sorry for what I said. I just lost my temper," muttered Ace.

"Now Michael, to answer your question," Belle went on to say, "We do have a hideout that is way out yonder in the hills. After your men get here tomorrow, all my men and that includes Dean will take you to our hide out. That a boy, Michael. Go after him. Get The Stunning Kid and then all's well that ends well.

Now that that is settled, why don't you come out in the saloon and we'll get you some vittles to eat and then we'll get you a room at the hotel."

Chapter 29

NOW WE HAVE DOUBLE TROUBLES

Stephen then climbed down from the saloon's roof and went over to The Marshal's Office. Once inside, he found Marshal Allen sitting at his desk and Hannibal sitting next to him.

"When did you two lawmen get back?" asked Stephen.

"Oh, about fifteen minutes ago," replied The Marshal.

"I was just telling the Marshal about John Wayne's movies," noted Hannibal. "Some of my favorite movies John Wayne made was Big Jake, The Horse Solders and probably his best one of all, True Grit."

"We could sure use John Wayne right now," reasoned Stephen as he explained to The Marshal and Hannibal what he overheard on the saloon roof over Dean's office.

"Now we've got double troubles. We not only have to deal with The Dean Dickerson Gang. Michael, The Magnificent is here in town. His gang will be here tomorrow afternoon. Michael, The Magnificent was hired by Belle to come to Dodge, to track down and kill The Stunning Kid."

Stephen then went on to explain how The Stunning Kid found Michael along the road with a broken leg and how he had Rex send him a doctor from the 21st century to set it and put it in a cast.

"I just think I made our job a lot tougher by helping Michael," Stephen blurted. "I fought a lot of good men in the boxing ring. I just couldn't leave Michael along the road to die. That's another fine mess I got us into. I don't think I can handle it."

"We need the cavalry to come to our rescue," reasoned Hannibal. "What you said about Rex sending you a doctor from the 21st century, I think we need to get Rex to send us the rest of The West Side Kids. In fact, let's ask Rex to bring us home so we can come up with our own plans.

Would you like to come with us Marshal? I'm sure you will find the 21st century very interesting. If you come, you will meet your great, great, great grandson. As long as were going, let's ask Oliver Columbo if he would like to come with us to meet his great, great, great grandson."

I think I would really like to see what the future is like," replied The Marshal. "You bet I'll go."

"We better go get Oliver Columbo and bring him here right away," replied Stephen. "If he comes back with us, will there be somebody there to take care of my horses until we get back?"

"Oh yes. Oliver has a stable hand that works for him," explained The Marshal.

Thirty minutes later, Oliver Columbo was at The Marshal's Office.

"Hello Oliver," greeted Marshal Allen. "You know these two men and why they're here from the 21st century. Would you like to go with us to the 21st century to meet your great, great, great grandson?"

"I'm more than ready," reasoned Oliver. "I have been talking to Hannibal and Stephen about the 21st century. I can't even imagine the things they have been telling me about the future. Now I'll get to see these things for myself."

"Just a word of caution," advised Stephen. "When you get to the future, there may be some things that you see that may frighten you. If that happens, don't be afraid to tell us about it. I need to write that down what I just said. I should be a writer."

"What did you say that was so brilliant, genius?" asked Hannibal.

"Oh, I said things that may frighten you. Don't be afraid," laughed Stephen.

"I think being The Stunning Kid is getting to be too much for you," Hannibal went on to say. "You're getting to sound more and more like Scooter."

"And what's wrong with that," smiled Stephen. "Scooter is OK. He makes me laugh a lot and helps me see the good things in life. He's your friend and my friend."

"I know," answered Hannibal. "I miss him too and in a few minutes were going to be with our friend Scooter."

"I miss him too," broke in Marshal Allen. "He's my friend too. I never meant anybody like him. He's one of a kind. OK boys. It's time to call out to Rex and in a few minutes we will all see Scooter again in the 21st century."

"Rex, oh Rex. If you can hear me, bring Hannibal and me home. We've got big problems and need your help. Marshal Allen and Oliver Columbo wants to come with us," instructed Stephen.

"I guess he didn't hear us," Hannibal went on to say as everybody disappeared out of The Marshal's Office.

Chapter 30

BACK TO THE 21ST CENTURY WE GO

Sixty seconds later, everybody appeared in Rex's Office.

"Hello boys," greeted Rex. "I see you have two passengers with you. One of them is Marshal Allen, my grandfather and the other one is Oliver Columbo, T. J.'s grandfather.

Hello grandfather," Rex continued to say as Detective T. J. Columbo came through the office door. "It's been a long time coming. I finally get to meet you."

"Hello grandson," replied Marshal Allen. "I've really been looking forward to meeting you. So you're a Police Detective?"

"Which one of you is my grandson?" asked Oliver Columbo.

"You're looking at him," answered T. J. "I'm also a Police Detective."

"Where is Scooter?" asked an anxious Hannibal. "Can I hire one of you Detectives to find him for me?"

"He's at the shooting range getting firearms and training drills," explained Rex. "He's going back to Dodge with us. He seems to need more practice with his firearms."

"You can say that again," insisted Stephen. "He went behind the stables in Dodge to practice shooting. He hit everything but the target. He even shot my hat off my head. When he has a gun in his hand, the safest place to stand is in front of him."

"Wait until you see him shoot now. He can even hit the target," promised Rex. "When he goes back to Dodge, now he can protect himself with the additional training he's getting."

"He's not going back to Dodge," ordered Hannibal. "Stephen, The Marshal and yours truly can't watch him all of the time. The Dean Dickerson Gang wants to kidnap him."

"Oh, we've got that covered," explained Rex. "The rest of The West Side Kids, Columbo and me are all going back together. With The Marshal and Oliver, that will make fourteen of us. Columbo has been training The West Side Kids in firearms, police techniques and training drills. They are ready to go.

T. J. Columbo's brother, Barney and my brother, Happy who both own pizza parlors are going back with us to cook for all of us. Now that will make sixteen of us.

I'm going to take on the role I had as The Captain in the navy and take charge as if all of you are recruits. There will be two squads of seven. I will be in charge of the first squad and T. J. Columbo will lead the second squad.

Since we may be outnumbered, each of us will take with us a concealed bullet proof vest, a 9mm semiautomatic pistol with a magazine that holds 18 rounds of ammunition and a two way radio."

"Rex, if you go, who is going to be helping Don with the time machine?" asked Stephen.

"My boss, Lieutenant Moe Mannix will be helping Don and his wife Cat with the time machine," answered Rex. "Don has a very nice motor home and a German Shepard. The German Shepard will be free to run around the farm. The three of them will be staying in the motor home taking turns monitoring the time machine."

"Guns that hold 18 bullets at a time, concealed bullet proof vests, two way radios, a motor home, whatever they are," remarked Oliver. "I can't believe what I'm hearing."

"That's right. These things would be strange to you grandfather," replied T. J. "It will be a couple of days before we all go to Dodge City. How would you and Rex's grandfather like us to include you in some of the police training and techniques while your here? Then we can take you to a nice restaurant to eat and give you a tour of our town and after that we will get both of you a room at a motel."

"What's a motel?" asked Oliver.

"All Hannibal keeps talking about is John Wayne, John Wayne. While we're here, can we see something called a movie about a John Wayne?" asked Marshal Allen. "I want to see why Hannibal likes this guy with the true grit and the patch over one eye riding on top of the stagecoach shooting Indians with a Winchester Rifle."

"Oh, you want to see the movies Stagecoach and True Grit," answered Rex. "Maybe you would like to see The Horse Solders, Chisum, Rooster Cogburn, McLintock and my favorite, Big Jake.

That's just a small handful of the movies he made. There was also a television series called Gunsmoke. It's about a U. S. Marshal called Matt Dillon that lives in Dodge City in your time period. You don't know it, but your going to be in for a treat. You will also get all of the rest of your questions answered while your here."

"What about my question concerning the time machine?" asked Stephen again.

"Oh yes," answered Rex. "You remember my boss, Lieutenant Moe Mannix. I explained to him about what were all into. He is very interested in what we're doing and will help us to man the time machine.

One last thing for now. When we all go to Dodge, we will all be going back as U. S. and Deputy Marshals. Along with Marshal Allen, Scooter and I will be Marshals and the rest of you will be Deputies."

"Scooters going to be a Marshal. Scooters is going to be a Marshal?" asked Hannibal. "Is that what you said or is there something wrong with my hearing?"

"Yes Hannibal, that's part of my plan that Scooter is going to be a Marshal," explained Rex. "I have to get him all the protection I can. A gang member by the name of Ace accidentally took Scooter's coin that Don gave him. After that he was transported here by the time machine. I sort of gave him the impression that Scooter was really the boss of you and Stephen.

I told him to look out for Scooter and if Scooter starts to shiver all over he can be very violent. Now to keep up with the lie I told Ace, Scooter has to go back as a U. S. Marshal."

"I guess that makes sense, but a Marshal?" reasoned Hannibal. "Oh yes, before I forget, I brought some bullets back with me that Stephen gave me to get annualized. We dug up the Marshal that was shot in the back and took this bullet out of him. I want to see if any of these bullets match the one from the Marshal. I also want you to have these hundred dollar bills checked out to see if any of them are counterfeit. Scooter, a U. S. Marshal?"

"That reminds me," Rex added to what he was saying. "I have a friend who is a real U. S. Marshal. He is going to have some badges made up of that time period, with the paperwork to give me. He is going to swear us all in and we're all going back as real Marshals.

Stephen since you and Hannibal are here, I want to take a day or two to teach you and Hannibal about police techniques before we go back. I don't want you or Hannibal to be trapped into being challenged to a gunfight. We may be going back to the old west. We're going to handle making arrests using the police techniques of the 21st century."

Chapter 31

MICHAEL, THE MAGNIFICENT TAKES OVER

As Rex and the boys prepare to go back to Dodge City in 1880, The Dean Dickerson Gang ride to their hideout in the hills with Michael, The Magnificence's Gang. Once inside the hideout cabin, Michael asks everybody to sit somewhere to listen to his plans.

"Here is how I plan on pulling jobs. I will explain everything to you," offered Michael. "There is an honest way and a sneaky way of doing things. My plan will always be the sneaky way."

"And just how does that happen?" asked Dean. "You sound as if your in a creative mood. Let's hear it and keep it sensible."

"This is the part I'm going to actually love," laughed Michael, The Magnificent. "The Stunning Kid seems to be protecting the helpless and the little guy who can't defend themselves. My plan is for The Stunning Kid and his gang to get blamed for all the robberies, hold ups and cattle rustling that we're going to do.

Nobody is going to trust The Stunning Kid anymore. If this doesn't keep The Stunning Kid busy avoiding the law and out of our hair, nothing will."

"I see what you mean. This has lots of possibilities," reasoned Dean. "If this is true, it would be a miracle. But The Stunning Kid doesn't have a gang."

"He does now," replied Michael. "I need to get a black horse like The Stunning Kids. Next, I need one of you who is the build of The Stunning Kid to dress in black with a Mexican hat and mask.

As The Stunning Kid. I want you to pull job after job as The Stunning Kid taking some of our men with you. As I said he will be blamed for all these robberies and a price will be placed on his head. Every lawman in the territory will be after him."

"That's a great idea," replied Dean. "I can get us a black horse. Which one of us is going to be The Stunning Kid?"

"You there. What's your name?" asked Michael. "You have the same build as The Stunning Kid."

"My name is Danny. You're saying you want me to be The Stunning Kid?" asked Danny.

"I don't know if you ever heard of if the shoe fits?" replied Michael. "You look like the right shoe. Danny, you will be our secret weapon by doing the actual fighting. I think you can make everybody believe you're The Stunning Kid."

"But I can't shoot as good as The Stunning Kid. I will be killed," cried Danny.

"You may think it isn't going to be easy. Don't worry about it Danny. You will do alright. I guarantee that you will be fine. All five of my men will be your gang and they can shoot. They are the best there is," explained Michael. "As of now we're not running. If the real Stunning Kid shows up, my men won't run. They will shoot The Stunning Kid. That's what Belle hired us to do."

"What other ideas did you have?" asked Lefty. "You said when we were in Dean's office you had a couple of ideas."

"That's right," answered Michael. "There is eight of you and six of us. Together we can rustle cattle and chase The homesteaders off of their land. Only were not going to be nice about it. We're all going to be Indians and we will burn down their cabins and their barns. We will also attack the stagecoach, the gold mines or anything we can make a buck on."

"I thought we were doing pretty good before. We're going to have one humdinger of a gang," reasoned Dean. "This is going to be a lot better than I ever imaged. You're really something else. Michael. You have a great head on your shoulders and are really a natural as a gang leader. Belle is going to really like this."

"Who needs Belle?' questioned Michael. "What good will she be?"

"Not so fast. You don't understand," explained Ace. "We need Belle. You'll see. If anybody can find out what jobs to pull Belle can. She is friends with The Mayor and The Banker and other important people who come into her saloon.

Belle is a good spy for the gang. She has a friendly smile and doesn't talk much. She does have a way to get the right people to tell her what she needs to know. They wouldn't come into her saloon if any of their wives had anything to do with it.

The talents each of us are going to use when we work together is what is going to make us the money. It's a good thing we're going into business together. If all of us work together, we will all get a larger slice of the pie. We're going to make a fortune and be real live millionaires"

"All right. I'm getting it. Just as I start rolling with my plans, you make sense about Belle. There is a first time for everything. I'll go along with that for now," offered Michael. "Me and my gang never depended on anybody else for pulling jobs before. Maybe this new arrangement will be a step up for all of us. I always believe in becoming the kind of leader that people would follow voluntarily, even if I don't have a tittle or position. I want it understood right now that I'm the boss and I will be reporting to Belle."

"Now wait a minute," boomed Dean. "I am the boss of my gang and you're not taking over."

"Listen to me. It makes no difference who you were. Yes, you will remain the boss of your gang and second in command," promised Michael. "I came up with ideas you never even thought of and you like them. The Stunning Kid has been giving you the problems. From now on we will be giving him the problems because of my plans. You will be reporting to me and doing what I say if you want to make this work. When I'm done, your gang will be better than new."

"Alright, that sounds good to me," answered Dean. "I think you and I better go see Belle and tell her of our new arrangements."

"No," responded Michael. "All of you said that somehow The Stunning Kid always knows what you're going to do before you do it.

Remember, it's not how good we are. It's how good we want to be. We need to come up with a strategy for each of these jobs that were going to pull or the execution will be worthless if The Stunning Kid interferes. And without the right execution, our strategy will be worthless.

Belle needs to come to our hide out to talk about our operation. We need to tighten up our security if we're going to outfox The Stunning Kid.

I'm going to take Danny with me to Twin Forks to get a black outfit. Dean, you take the rest of the gang in to Dodge and find the outfits we need to have to be Indians. Bring back that black stallion and Belle here at the hide out in two days. When Belle gets here, she will find out I'm going to be the brains and boss of this outfit."

"Belle isn't going to like that one bit," insisted Dean. "This is her gang, her operation and we take orders from her. She just isn't going to stand for it."

"There is nothing she can do about it. I'm afraid she doesn't have any choice," explained Michael. "Belle agreed in front of everybody that I can work on my plan with no strings attached. If she wants me to keep my end of the bargain, she needs to hold up her end of the bargain. This is not about how bad she wants me to pay off the debt I owe her. It's about how hard she is willing to work with me to get my debt paid off to her.

As we all know, I'm in a bind and Belle won't help me out. She insists that I pay my debt to her instead of The Stunning Kid and that put her in a bind. Who would she want me to pay my debt to, her or The Stunning Kid?"

"It looks like things are starting to get nasty for Belle if she puts up a fight," reasoned Dean. "The best choice is for Belle to go along with you, Michael. She may agree not to be the top boss anymore if she understands how we're going to run the gang and how that will benefit all of us."

"Give Belle time and she will see the benefits," replied Michael. "I'm only doing this to solve Belle's problems and make us all some money. Now I suggest you take the men and go to Dodge. I'll see you in a couple of days."

"OK men. You heard him. Let's get ready and go to Dodge to get the supplies we need," ordered Dean.

Two days later, Danny and Michael was back at the hide out with a Stunning Kid outfit. Dean and the gang returned to the hide out with Belle, a black stallion, and the outfits for the gang to be Indians.

"OK men and Belle sit down so we can talk about the next things we need to do," Michael began to say. "I decided to call our reign of terror as, Hasta la Vista Stunning Kid. Belle, I've got you here for a reason.

The first thing I need to explain to you about my plan is who is going to be the top boss. You expect me to pay my debt to you by getting rid of The Stunning Kid. We both agreed for me to do this with no strings attached. Because I have the ideas, the right men and the capability, I am going to be the top boss."

"I just heard what you were doing before I came to the hide out. I hired you to get rid of The Stunning Kid, not take over my organization," objected Belle.

"Listen to me Belle, my ideas won't work unless you agree with me about being the top boss," insisted Michael. "I not only can get rid of The Stunning Kid, I can make all of us a ton of money."

"I don't know," replied Belle. "I started this gang and we were doing really good until The Stunning Kid showed up. We got rid of the Marshal who was giving us all the trouble and made Rocky Allen, the town drunk, Marshal.

He fooled us and brought in three capable Deputies to help him clean up this town. I take that back. Two capable Deputies and one who is always lost in thought. When you get rid of The Stunning Kid, things will go better for our gang."

"That's what I'm trying to do is make things better for our gang. I've got something to tell you Belle. This is going to be how things are going to work. A boss has the tittle. A leader has the people. Because I have the people, I'm taking over," insisted Michael.

"I don't know how you figure and I don't think that I like that," stated Belle. "Maybe your trying to help me. Maybe you're trying to help yourself."

"I was wondering when you was going to ask that question," reasoned Michael. "It's no use getting hostile about it. Belle, if you haven't found this out yet, the problem with being the strong one or the top boss is that no one offers to give you a hand when you need it. I'm not going to take the time to argue with you. I'm not going to pull a fast one and double cross everyone. You have my word on it.

If you have any more objections to this arrangement, I'll have to forget about paying my debt to you by honoring my debt to The Stunning Kid. Now tell me, which choice would be your pleasure and I will honor it?"

"If I go with your plan to make you the top boss. What will Dean's job and my job be?" asked Belle.

"You both will continue to be the boss of your gang," explained Michael. "The only difference is that your gang is to come to me to work out the execution and the strategy of any jobs we pull.

Now that The Stunning Kid is going to have a gang of his own and the settlers are going to have to deal with renegade Indians. The strategy and execution has to be perfect."

"Now that you explained this new operation to me, I can see the advantages of working together," reasoned Belle. "OK, I will agree to do that. Now let's move on. What do we do next?"

"First of all, I couldn't find an ideal costume in Twin Forks for Danny to be The Stunning Kid," explained Michael.

"I could hardly wait for you to talk about that," said an excited Dean. "Ace and I have that problem solved. I noticed a black stallion at Oliver Columbo's stable. Ace and I have had our eye on him for the last couple of days. I thought the horse belonged to Oliver, so Ace and I went to his stable to purchase the horse.

Oliver was nowhere to be found. According to the stable hand, Oliver left town a couple days ago. The stable hand has no idea where Oliver went or when he would be back. The stable hand sold me the black stallion for $75.00 saddle and all.

Ace and I was very surprised what we found when we went through the saddle bags."

"Well, what did you find in the saddle bags?" questioned Michael. "How does that solve my problem finding a costume?"

"It was a humdinger what we found in the saddle bags. We've got something to show you. Look it's The Stunning Kid's costume, guns and all," explained Dean. "Whoever owns the black stallion and all this gear is The Stunning Kid. What a find."

"I think today's the day that this looks like the beginning and end of The Stunning Kid. That solves your problem as well Danny. You don't have to worry about The Stunning Kid coming after you. He has disappeared as if he was an invisible man," said a surprised Michael. "Dean, get the costume for Danny to try on while the rest of us discuss our first job."

"Now that I think about it," recalled Lefty. "I haven't seen The Marshal or his Deputy's around Dodge for a couple of days."

"I haven't seen The Marshal and his Deputy's either," said Mugs.

"Me either," said Shorty.

"That's strange," replied Belle. "I don't know what's going on here. I haven't seen them either."

"I don't know what they're up to," exclaimed Michael. "I don't think there is anything to worry about. There are too many of us for The Marshal and his Deputy's to give us any trouble. Whoever The Stunning Kid was, he isn't about to give us any more trouble."

"I have just the job for The Stunning Kid and his gang to pull," suggested Belle. "The Golden Moon Mine is sending another shipment of gold on the stage tomorrow morning."

"That's good ole Belle for you," praised Dean. "It looks like our gang is back in action without the interference of The Stunning Kid or The Marshal."

"OK gang. Here's what we're going to do tomorrow to get that money," explained Michael. "There won't be a slip up because all fourteen of us will be in on the job. The stagecoach driver and whoever is riding as shotgun will only see Danny and my five men. The rest of you will follow as a backup, for just in case. Who has an idea as to where we can ambush the stage?"

"I do," volunteered Mugs. "I think the best place to hit the stage is at Twin Rocks."

"OK gang let's get things started by using strategy and execution," ordered Michael. "Mugs and Shorty take Belle back to Dodge. While your back in town, look to see if The Marshal and his Deputies are back in town. If they're not, the territory will be wide open. Belle, you start working extra hard to find other jobs for us.

After we rob the stage tomorrow, I want to start our raids as Indians and then continue to have The Stunning Kid and his gang pull one job after another. Everybody who lives in this territory will be so scared that they will be afraid of their own shadows.

The rest of us are riding to Twin Rocks to plan our strategy and execution for tomorrow. The gold shipment from The Golden Moon Mine is already ours."

"Michael, if The Marshal and his Deputies come back to Dodge, Stephen Edwards is someone else we will have to deal with," added Ace.

"The Stunning Kid, Stephen Edwards, it doesn't make any difference to me. If either one of them try to get in our way, it will be their last time," promised Michael. "Just let them try. I just hope they do. Make sure all of you get to bed early tonight. Make sure you wake up rested and sober. Tomorrow is our big day and we're starting very early."

Chapter 32

THE PRECIOUS GOLDEN MOON MINE SHIPMENT

It was finally 7 a. m. The next morning and the stage with the gold from The Golden Moon Mine was pulling out of town with one person named Denver, riding shotgun to protect the gold.

"I wish we had more men riding with us on this trip. We're hauling precious cargo," said the driver to Denver. "I would even be happy if we had John Wayne with us."

"Who is John Wayne?" asked Denver.

"Don't you know who he is?" asked the driver.

"No, I never heard of him," replied Denver. "Who is he?"

"Well pilgrim. I don't know who he is. I just was told by one of The Deputy Marshals he is one of the roughest, toughest hombres there is," explained the driver.

"The Deputy told me that this John Wayne sat on top of a stagecoach with a tribe of Indians chasing it. He used a Winchester to hold off the Indians until the cavalry came to the rescue. If anybody has it, he does."

"Has what?" asked Denver.

"You know, true grit. I guess he is very famous for true grit and he is known the world over," explained the driver. "As he's gotten older, he wears a patch over one eye."

"You don't say. If he's so famous, why haven't I ever heard of him?" exclaimed Denver.

"I don't know. I just don't know," replied the driver. "We've been on the road for ten minutes. We better keep our eyes open. In fifteen minutes, we'll be approaching Twin Rocks. I'll feel better after we get past Twin Rocks."

Fifteen minutes later, the stagecoach was approaching Twin Rocks. As the stage got closer, The Stunning Kid and five masked members of his gang rode out from behind the rocks in front of the stagecoach. As the driver stopped the coach, a frightening look appeared on the faces of both men sitting up on the stage. Eight more masked riders rode out from behind the rocks in back of the stage.

"As you can see, this is a holdup. Throw your guns on the ground now or you won't even live to regret it," ordered The Stunning Kid. "Now throw down the strongbox full of gold."

"It's The Stunning Kid," said the driver to Denver. "It's not worth our lives to put up a fight."

"I thought The Stunning Kid worked alone helping the underdog," insisted Denver. "He doesn't rob stages."

"In a pig's eye. There's no money in helping the underdog. I never could stand those rascals and because of that I have changed my mind," replied The Stunning Kid. "I have to eat. From now on, I'm thinking of number one, me. Only me. Now that I have my own gang, nobody, but nobody is going to stand in my way. Next time you see The Marshal, you tell him what I said. It goes for him as well.

Next, I want your four passengers to get out of the coach, because everybody is going to contribute to our gang, including you two."

Ace climbed down from his horse, took off his hat and walked up to the passengers.

"Put all your contributions in my hat," ordered Ace. "You lady, take that ring off of your finger and put it in my hat."

"My grandmother gave me this ring. It belonged to her grandmother. Please don't take it," pleaded the lady to The Stunning Kid. "I'm a school teacher in Dodge City. All the kids idolize what you do, helping the innocent and helpless. Make this awful man let me keep my ring."

"I'm sorry lady. Tell your brats to idolize somebody else," answered The Stunning Kid. "Me and my men are here to rob the stage, not to be nice about it."

"You heard him. Now give me your ring or do you want me to cut it off your finger?" asked Ace as he pulled out a very large knife.

"No, take it," cried the lady. "It looks like everybody in the territory is going to be after The Stunning Kid. Stephen Edwards especially."

"Thank you for your contributions. Everybody can get back into the coach," instructed Rex. "Now that we have the gold, be on your way. I'm very sure we'll meet again."

The gang began yelling and shooting their guns in the air. The driver took the whip to the team of horses and away he went.

"That holdup went very well," praised Michael to his gang. "See how strategy and execution works when you do it properly. Everything was very smooth. We didn't have to chase the stagecoach to get the gold and we got the gold without anybody giving us any trouble. Nobody got hurt except for The Stunning Kid's reputation.

Dean and I are going to Dodge to report to Belle and see if she has any other jobs we can do. I don't think we quite broke the spirit of what people think of The Stunning Kid. It will take a couple more jobs and The Stunning Kid will no longer be everybody's hero."

"How am I doing so far?" asked Danny.

"Danny, you did a great job as The Stunning Kid and if you continue to do a good job, you will have a great reputation with the gang," answered Michael. "We need to find another job right away. I can hardly wait to see how Danny portrays The Stunning Kid on the next job.

Now everybody, let's go back to the hide out and celebrate the hold up and Danny. He gave a great performance as The Stunning Kid."

Chapter 33

THE STAGE WAS HELD UP

Two hours later the stage pulled into Twin Forks with the driver yelling, "The stage was held up. The stage was held up.'"

Hearing the driver yell, the Sheriff of Twin Forks ran out of his office and over to the stage depot where a crowd of townspeople formed.

"Who did it? Was anybody hurt?" asked Sheriff Gold.

"It was The Stunning Kid and his gang!" exclaimed Denver. "There was at least forty of them and I couldn't do anything to stop them."

"If John Wayne had been riding shotgun, he would have stopped them," replied the driver.

"All I've heard on this trip is John Wayne, John Wayne. Next time get John Wayne to ride shotgun," ordered Denver.

"Who is this John Wayne?" asked Sheriff Gold.

"He is the most famous, roughest, toughest hombre in the west. He wears a patch over one eye and has true grit," explained the driver.

"I never heard of this John Wayne. As far as The Stunning Kid goes, I have heard of him and I happen to know he works alone. I don't believe he has a gang," reasoned The Sheriff.

"There is no mistake. It was The Stunning Kid alright, only there was about fourteen or fifteen altogether who held us up. Not forty," explained the driver.

"Where did the gang stop you?" asked The Sheriff.

"We were stopped at Twin Rocks just outside Dodge," replied the driver. "The gold from The Golden Moon Mine was stolen."

"Why didn't you go back to Dodge and report the holdup to The Marshal?" asked Sheriff Gold.

"Nobody has seen The Marshal and his Deputies for a couple of days. Nobody knows where they went or when they will be back," answered Denver. "So we thought it was best to come to Twin Forks."

"Sheriff Gold, those bandits were so mean that they took the ring that my grandmother gave me," cried the school teacher. "Please, please help me get it back."

"It may be too late to track them down. I'm going to form a posse and go after them," yelled Sheriff Gold. "I want everybody who can ride and shoot to meet me over at my office in ten minutes and I will swear you all in as Deputies."

"If you can get me a horse, I will go," volunteered the driver.

"Since there was only fifteen in the gang, I'll go," snorted Denver. "If there was forty of them like I though, I would have to think about it."

"I have two extra horses," said a rancher in the crowd.

"OK. Bring plenty of ammunition and get over to my office in a hurry. We've lost too much time already," reckoned The Sheriff.

Chapter 34

ROBBING THE CATTLEMAN'S BANK

Later that afternoon, Dean and Michael returned to the hide out where everybody was celebrating.

"Look at our gang," said Dean to Michael. "It's been a while since they have had something to celebrate. I have to hand it to you the way you think."

"Thank you for the compliment," replied Michael. "Now we have to prepare for another job that Belle gave us to do. Let's join in the celebration and later we'll get everybody together to plan our next job, which is to rob The Cattleman's Bank in Dodge.

After a brief meeting, I want you and a couple of men to go into Dodge to plan our strategy for tomorrow. While were there, we need to find out if The Marshal and his Deputies came back."

It was finally 8:45 a. m. the next morning. The gang entered Dodge in groups of twos from different directions, going into Belle's Saloon for a quick drink. As the clock ticked away, it was now 9:00 a. m. and The Cattleman's Bank opened their doors with The Stunning Kid, with five of his gang entered the bank, with guns drawn while the other nine members of the gang remained outside watching for trouble.

"This is a hold up," announced The Stunning Kid. "The bank down the street recommended that we come to see you and remove your money by the way of the front door. I would be delighted if all of you behind the counter would walk over facing that wall with your hands up while we relieve you of all your money. I do require the services of The Bank President to open up the vault."

"If I live and breathe, you're The Stunning Kid," replied The Bank President.

"Yeah, yeah, yeah, I know who I am," replied The Stunning Kid. "What of it? If you want to continue to breath, you better do what your told."

"What are you doing robbing a bank?" asked The Bank President. "You don't rob banks. Don't do this. What are people going to say? Everyone knows that you help people in your own way."

"That's right," answered The Stunning Kid. "Now I'm helping me in my own way. I mean business and if any of you get in my way, I'm going to let you have it. From now on, I'm only thinking of me, me, me. Get that vault door open and then get out of my way. I want that money, all that money in the vault. Do you understand?"

"If you do this, you're going to disappoint everybody in the territory. Stop this right now," ordered The Bank President.

"Get out of my way old man," demanded The Stunning Kid as he pushed The Bank President down on the floor.

As The Bank President laid on the floor, he reached over to a shelf under the counter for a gun and was then shot by The Stunning Kid.

"Don't anybody else try that. It's not worth dying for." ordered The Oklahoma Kid with both guns drawn and cocked. "We don't want to hurt anybody else. We came just for the money."

"We got it all. Let's get out of here," yelled The Stunning Kid as he ran out the front door to Thunder. "Mount up and ride."

A half hour later, the gang was back at the hideout celebrating and drinking whiskey.

"We sure had another successful hold up. Let's make a toast to Michael," said Danny to the gang holding up his glass of whiskey in the air. "I saw all the storekeepers looking out their windows. They were all afraid to challenge us."

"Thank you all," exclaimed Michael. "Let's continue to put the pressure on the territory. In a half hour, I want everyone dressed as Indians. We're going to raid The Wilson Homestead next."

Chapter 35

THE TIME TRAVELING MARSHALS GO TO DODGE

Meanwhile back in the 21st century Rex, Moe Mannix, Don, and his time machine, Columbo and the rest of the gang was back on the farm where this adventure began.

Everyone was outfitted in their ten gallon hats, cowboy boots, holsters with 9mm pistols and concealed bulletproof vests under their western shirts. Other equipment the U. S. Marshals was issued was two way radios, AR 15 rifles and 12 gauge semi-automatic pump shotguns.

Everyone was also assigned horses with western saddles. Barney and Happy, who was going to cook for the new Marshals was each given a covered wagon full of food, with a team of horses.

"Now that were all together and ready to go, does anybody have any questions?" asked Rex.

"I do," answered Scooter.

"You might know it would be you Scooter. What do you have to know?" questioned Rex.

"When are we going to eat?" asked Scooter.

"It's going to be a while," answered Rex. "You should be fine. You just had a big lunch before we left Davenport and you ate like a pig."

"We'll I'm still hungry," replied Scooter.

"That reminds me," explained Scotter. "Three weeks ago, I was visiting a friend of mine in Chicago."

"Oh, you mean Blinky?" asked Hannibal.

"Yeah, yeah, yeah, Blinky is right," answered Scooter. "It was a Saturday and time for lunch. We were both very hungry. Blinky decided to take me to this very fancy restaurant in Chicago. Blinky had a suit on with a tie. I was wearing just a sport shirt."

"Didn't you have any pants on?" questioned Hanibal. "I suppose because of that, they wouldn't let you in the restaurant."

"Very funny Hannibal. Of course I did,"answered Scooter. "You needed a tie to get in the restaurant. I just didn't have on a tie. The Matradee took his tie off and gave it to me. After Blinky and I was sitting at a table, The Matradee asked me what I wanted to eat. I told him that I wanted a ham sandwich and a beer. The Matradee asked me to show him my drivers license. When he looked at my license, he found out I was only twenty years old and told me I wasn't old enough to get served a beer. I replied back to The Matradee that if he didn't get me a beer, I would tell everybody he wasn't wearing a tie and then he would get kicked out of the restaurant. What I said didn't work because I didn't get a beer."

"I don't know what I'm going to do with you. Get on your horse and get ready to go back in time," ordered Rex as his brother Don hit the button on the time machine.

Seconds later, The Marshals was sitting on the same hill above the same road as Stephen, Hannibal and Scooter appeared in the beginning of this adventure.

"Stephen, I better tell you before we go into Dodge about which bullet matched the one you took out of The Marshal's back," explained Rex.

"It was Ace's bullet. I just knew it," broke in Stephen.

"That was Ace's bullet and those $100.00 bills were counterfeit," stated Rex. "Which way is Dodge City?"

"After we ride down the hill and reach the road, we need to go to our right," instructed Stephen.

"OK Marshal," said Hannibal to Scooter as he began to laugh. "Lead the charge to Dodge City."

"That's a good idea," exclaimed Rex. "Scooter, you and Marshal Allen ride in front of all of us to make it look good. The sooner we get to Dodge, the sooner we can all eat."

"Well then let's go Mr. Dillon. If I'm in front, I'll be first in line to get something to eat," reasoned Scooter.

"Scooter, will you stop worrying about eating and get serious about what we're here to do," instructed Hannibal. "You know that Dean and his gang would like to get their hands on you, so don't do anything stupid and quite worrying about eating. As long as you stay with the group, you should be safe."

"If Dean and his gang capture Scooter, they're the ones who are going to need protection from Scooter. He will be blowing up things and turning the gang into little people," laughed Rex.

"Very funny Rex. You're never going to let me forget about that are you?" replied Scooter. "You do a couple of stupid things and you're branded for life."

"I know Scooter can do some strange things. What was it that Scooter did that you guys keep talking about?" asked Marshal Allen.

"Yes, I would like to know," chimed in Oliver Columbo.

"I'll tell you what he did," replied Rex as he began to tell the story beginning in chemistry class.

Fifteen minutes later The Marshals enter the city limits and are riding towards The Marshal's office as Rex finished his story. Finally, The Marshal's reach The Marshal's Office as a group of people walk towards The Marshals.

"Marshal Allen, Marshal Allen, where have you been?" asked one of the employees of The Cattleman's Bank. "Our bank was robbed this morning and the stage hauling the gold from Golden Moon Mine yesterday."

"Does anybody have any idea who did that?" asked Marshall Allen.

"There is no doubt about it," answered the bank employee. "It was The Stunning Kid."

"Did I hear you right? Did you say The Stunning Kid?" asked Stephen.

"You heard right. He now has a gang of about fourteen people who is pulling these jobs with him," explained the bank employee.

"Impossible, I know for a fact that it can't be," said a confused Stephen.

"We have several witness' that will tell you different," reasoned the bank employee.

"They even took the ring that my grandmother gave me, and I want it back," informed the school teacher who was riding the stage just as the fifteen year old Wilson boy rode up to The Marshals.

"Marshal Allen, Marshal Allen, Indians are attacking our homestead! My dad and mom are trying to hold them off! Please come now!" yelled the frantic boy.

Chapter 36

THE MARSHALS TO THE RESCUE

"OK gang. This is our first job and it's time to go. Barney and Happy, you stay here and go with Oliver Columbo to his stables," ordered Rex. "Everybody else follow Marshal Allen. Let's ride."

Twenty minutes later, the band of new Marshals saw the house and barn on fire as they approached The Wilson Homestead.

"I don't see any Indians," exclaimed Rex. "I think we can save the house if we put out the fire now. The barn is too far gone."

Just as the lawmen rode up to the pump in front of the house, Chester and Nora Wilson walked out of the draw alongside of the house.

"Marshal, thank God your here," yelled Chester in a joyous voice. "Nora, it looks like our house is going to be saved."

Just as everybody dismounted from their horses Hannibal yelled, "OK West Side Kids, Let's do the double play and get this fire out."

The boys quickly formed two lines with Who and I Don't Know at the pump. Ten minutes later the fire was out.

"I sure want to thank everybody for saving our house. We just can't thank you enough," praised Mr. Wilson. "Mrs. Wilson and I thought our house was a goner."

"We're glad we were available to help," replied Marshal Allen. "I thought there wasn't any Indians around for miles. Just who are these Indians your son was telling us about?"

"They wasn't from any tribe that I know about," explained Mr. Wilson. "They really didn't act like you would expect Indians to act. All we know is that there was about fourteen of them. Mrs. Wilson and I was lucky enough just to escape into the draw."

"Which way did they go? Did they go that away?" asked Rex. "I've always wanted to say that."

"They all rode towards the east. Why is it that you wanted to say what you just said?" asked Mr. Wilson.

"You wouldn't understand," answered Rex. "Columbo, why don't you take your squad and help Mr. and Mrs. Wilson clean up. The Indians might come back. If they do, contact us by radio. I'll take the rest of the men with me to go find these Indians. If I do I will contact you. It's 1:00 p. m. now. Get back to town before dark."

Chapter 37

WHERE IS THUNDER

It's 6:00 p. m. now and everybody is back at The Marshals Office where Barney is greeting the gang.

"We have a campfire behind the stable and Happy is there waiting to serve supper to all you superheroes. Come and get it right now," requested Barney.

"Finally, I get to eat. I'm on my way," announced Scooter.

"I think we're all ready to eat," commented Columbo. "It's been a long day."

"I'm anxious to go see Thunder and Lightning," added Stephen. "You know, I really missed them."

"Don't forget to take care of your horses," instructed Oliver. "They also need to eat and drink. You also have to take off their saddles and brush them down."

"Horses are like mirrors. Horses will show you back whatever you show them," beamed Stephen. "When you watch how a man treats his horse, you will see what's inside a man. I'm going to take care of my horses before I eat."

"They should be just fine. You eat while everything is hot," explained Oliver. "Then you can spend the rest of the night taking care of them."

The gang then went outside and mounted on their horses and rode to the stable. Once inside, Stephen began to look for his horses. He could only find Lightening. Thunder was nowhere to be found.

"Oliver, Oliver, I can't find Thunder. Where is he?" said Stephen in a desperate voice.

"He can't be far away. I'll ask my stable hand about Thunder," replied Oliver.

A couple of minutes later, Oliver found the stable hand and asked, "I had a big black Stallion I was boarding here. Where is he?"

"I thought that black stallion belonged to you," explained the stable hand. "Dean Dickerson came by a day or two after you left and he offered me $75.00, so I sold him the stallion. I thought you would be happy with the deal I made with Dean Dickerson."

"Well, I'm not," answered Oliver. "That horse was not mine to sell. I've got to get him back. Stephen, oh Stephen, I have to talk to you and Rex."

"What happened? Where's Thunder?" asked a frantic Stephen.

"What's wrong?" asked Rex.

"I've got some bad news for Stephen about Thunder," replied Oliver.

"Is Thunder OK? Where is Thunder?" questioned Stephen.

"While I was gone, my stable hand sold Thunder with your saddle and all your gear to Dean Dickerson for $75.00," answered Oliver. "He thought that stallion belonged to me."

"You know what that means. They not only have Thunder, they have The Stunning Kid's outfit," explained Rex. "That explains The Stunning Kid and the robberies."

"I don't care about The Stunning Kid's outfit," cried Stephen. "I just want Thunder back. I don't know who is riding Thunder. He just better not be mistreating him. I'm going over to Belle's Saloon right now, to find Dean Dickerson."

"Hold on there," ordered Rex. "Since you and my grandfather, Marshal Allen are in my squad, I am taking my squad over to Belle's Saloon to find this Dean Dickerson. When we get there, let me do the talking."

Ten minutes later, Rex and his squad was inside Belle's Saloon. Rex walked up to the bar and boomed, "Bar keep, where is Dean Dickerson?"

"What have we got here," answered the bar keeper. "Are you all Marshals? Where is Marshal Allen?"

"I asked you where Dean Dickerson is?" repeated Rex as he pulled out his 9 mm pistol from his holster and pointed it at the bar keep. "I'm not going to ask you again."

"You can't come in here and ask me a question and then pull a gun on me," said the bar keep.

"That's what you think. You have ten seconds to tell me. I'm waiting," ordered Rex as Belle was coming down the steps.

"Dean isn't here. I don't see him very often anymore," replied the bar keep.

"What's going on here?" demanded Belle. "My name is Belle and I own this saloon. You can't come into my saloon and threaten my employees just because you're the law. I'm going to report you to Marshal Allen. This is his town and not yours."

"So, you're the famous Belle I've been hearing about," replied Rex. "Marshal Allen and all of us are U. S. Marshals and we are all working together. I know all about you and your employees and none of them are upstanding citizens.

Dean Dickerson bought a black stallion from Oliver Columbo's stable hand for $75.00. Oliver wants the stallion back because it wasn't his to sell."

"That black horse belonged to an outlaw by the name of The Stunning Kid," explained Belle. "We not only have his horse; we have his saddle and his outfit. We did the law a favor by taking these things away from him."

"Who has his belongings now?" asked Rex. "That person is posing as The Stunning Kid and has robbed a stagecoach and a bank."

"Dean doesn't have the horse and all the belongings anymore. He sold it all to some guy for $200.00," Belle continued to say.

"Where is this Dean Dickerson? I want to talk to him," demanded Rex.

"I couldn't tell you. He doesn't work for me anymore," roared Belle.

"If you see him, you send him over to The Marshal's office," ordered Rex. "We need to get that stallion back. We're going to get that stallion back. Do you understand me?"

"I understand," replied Belle with a quiver in her voice.

"You better understand, and you better do what your told," boomed Rex. "I won't have any second thoughts about putting a woman in our jail. Come on boys. Let's go back to the office."

After The Marshals left, Belle said to the bar keep, Eddie. "I'm riding out to the hide out to tell Dean and Michael about these Marshals. Go saddle my horse while I go change my clothes."

"But Belle, it's really dark out there. Can't it wait until morning?" asked Eddie.

"We have got big troubles and I need to go now. I also need you to go with me," said an anxious Belle.

A couple minutes later, Rex and his squad was back at the stables.

"What did you find out Rex?" asked Columbo.

"I talked to Belle about Dean Dickerson buying the black stallion," answered Rex. "She said that Dean Dickerson didn't work for her anymore and she didn't know the whereabouts of the black stallion. She said Dean Dickerson sold the stallion to a stranger for $200.00.

I left Marshal Allen, Who, What, and Because staking out the saloon. If they need us, they will call us on their two way radios."

Ten minutes later, Marshal Allen was on the radio calling, "Rex, Rex, can you hear me? Over."

"Yes Grandfather," answered Rex. "I can hear you. Over."

"Belle and her bar keep just came out of the saloon and are riding out of town," replied Marshal Allen. "Do we follow? Over."

"Yes Grandfather. Keep your distance and watch for any trap. I think tonight's the night we're going to get some answers," instructed Rex. "We don't know the layout of the land. It's going to be too dark for the rest of us to follow tonight. Find out what you can and then get back to Dodge. Over."

"Yes Grandson. We'll be careful," insisted Marshal Allen. Over and out."

"Columbo, let's have the boys find a place in the stable to settle down for the night," instructed Rex. "We better have the boys taking turns being on guard. I don't know what to expect, but it's better to be prepared."

"I agree with you about that one. Because we're in a different time and a different place, we better be prepared. It's a good thing we trained the men for this," explained Columbo. "I'll make the assignments to the men."

Chapter 38

THE SEARCH BEGINS

It was 6:00 a. m. the next morning as the smell of bacon and coffee filled the air.

"OK boys, it's time to rise and shine!" yelled Happy as he rang the bell to summon the sleeping Marshals. "It's time to get up and eat. The day is half over."

As everybody sat up, they yawned and rubbed their eyes except for Scooter. He quickly stood up and ran over to the chuck wagon.

"I'm very hungry and first in line!" yelled Scooter.

"You didn't wash up," scolded Barney. "You don't eat until you wash up."

Scooter quickly ran over to the other covered wagon to get some water to wash his hands and face. A couple minutes later he was back in line at the chuck wagon, only he was last in line. Everybody else was ahead of him in line.

"Grandfather, what was you able to find out?" questioned Rex.

"Well Grandson, we was able to follow Belle into the hills for a ways and then we lost her in the dark," explained Marshal Allen. "I think she knows where Dean Dickerson is and went to warn him about you."

"I'm sure of it," replied Rex. "I think we need to have the boys staking out Belle's Saloon twenty four hours a day until something else turns up."

"I have an idea," insisted Stephen. "Why not let me, Hannibal and Scooter go with Marshal Allen into the hills where he lost Belle. We all know the territory by now. Maybe we'll turn up something. I want to get Thunder back. If we need help, we can always call you on the radio."

"You can go, but I'm going with you," answered Rex. "Just for extra security, we'll take Who and Because with us.

Columbo, since I'm going with my squad to look for Thunder, take the rest of the boys and split up in two groups and patrol Dodge. All of you may be in danger. Make sure everyone is wearing their bullet proof vest."

"Stephen, before you go, I have something to show you, Hannibal and Scooter," beamed Oliver. "Rex, would you let me talk to your men for about fifteen minutes. I've got something to show these boys. In fact, maybe the whole gang would like to come out to the coral behind the stables. Stephen, because my stable hand sold Thunder to Dean Dickerson, I feel responsible for your loss. I've been thinking about it and I'm going to try and make it up to you the best I know how."

Now that we're here at my coral, I want to show you two well marked Palominos I own. I'm going to let you pick one out and he's yours. The other one I'm going to give to Hannibal. When you go back to the 21st century, you can take them with you."

"Thank you, Oliver. That is very thoughtful of you," praised Stephen. "That one over by the gate is the one I want. He looks just like Trigger, Roy Roger's horse."

"I know," replied Oliver. "When I went back to the 21st century, I got to see what you call it, a DVD of one of Roy Rogers movies called Heldorado? That's what made me think of my stallions."

"I don't know what to say," replied Stephen. "I think I'll name him Columbo in honor of you."

"That's very nice of you son. Since he looks like Trigger, I think a better name for him would be Trigger," reasoned Oliver.

"Thank you, Oliver for my Palomino," said an excited Hannibal. "I never had a horse of my own. All I ever ride is my motorcycle. I think I'm going to name my horse Tarzan."

"Scooter don't look so sad. I didn't forget you. I saved the best for last.

I understand that women don't like you," laughed Oliver. "I have the solution for that. You see Mischief in the corner of the coral. She's yours if you want her."

"That's a donkey, not a horse," roared Scooter. "You mean to tell me that Stephen and Hannibal each get a Palomino and I get a donkey?"

"No son. Mischief is a mule and if you take care of her, she will always love you," answered Oliver. "She is my very own personal mule. I wouldn't give her up to anyone but you. I trust you very much and I know you will be very kind to her, and you will take care of her."

"Do you really mean it?" asked an excited Scooter. "Is she really mine?"

"She sure is," replied Oliver. "If you really want her, I'll saddle her up and you can take her with you when you go look for Thunder."

"I don't know how to thank you. I just don't know how to thank you," boomed Scooter. "Did you hear that Hannibal? I have a real mule. She's all mine. I'll never ever forget you for this Oliver, never."

"That's OK son. Just seeing the instant love you have for Mischief makes it worth giving her to you," reasoned Oliver. "Having the privilege of you being in my life and knowing you will always love her is my reward in letting you have her."

Chapter 39

Back At The Hide Out

As the boys are getting their new mounts saddled and preparing to leave town, Michael is at the hide out talking to Belle and the gang about the new Marshals in Dodge.

"It looks like that new Marshal Rex knows what he's doing," insisted Michael. "Belle be advised: Because of your lack of planning, it created an emergency for you to ride to the hide out right away. I'm sure you was being watched by The Marshals and they followed you out of town."

"How did you know Michael?" asked Belle.

"It sounds like the Marshal has a strategy and execution of his own and you reacted to it," explained Michael. "That's something you better be doing with these Marshals or they're going to get the best of you.

When you go back to Dodge, be nice to the Marshals and don't give them any reason to harass you. Just as they are trying to get information out of you, lead them on. If you're really nice to them, they may slip up and tell you what you want to know."

"Because The Marshals know somebody has the black stallion, they must realize that person also has The Stunning Kids outfit," insisted Danny. "Am I going to pull any more jobs as The Stunning Kid?"

"Yes Danny. We're going to avoid contact with The Marshals by working the other towns in the territory by using strategy and execution," explained Michael. "The next town we're going to hit is Twin Forks."

"What about Marshal Gold in Twin Forks?" asked Lefty. "Will we have to fight him?"

"No, we won't," replied Michael. "My gang and I lived in Twin Forks for two months and we know the town very well. I'm going to draw a detailed map of Twin Forks and we can work out our strategy from the map. I already have a plan.

Belle, you and Eddie head back to Dodge right away. It won't look good if any of us ride back with you. Along the way, cut down the telegraph wires going from Dodge to Twin Forks."

Chapter 40
Looking For Thunder

As Michael and the gang worked on the strategy for Twin Forks, Belle and Eddie rode out from the hide out down the rocky hill to the road. In the distance Rex and his Deputies could see the duo.

As Belle and Eddie rode up to the Deputies, Belle went on to say, "Fancy meeting you here. Are you lost?"

"No, we're not lost," answered Rex. "After my talk with you last night, I was looking for you and I expected to find you out this way."

"Really," answered Belle, "It is very nice it is to see you again. How did you know I was out for a morning ride? It was so nice out this morning that I asked Eddie if he would go with me for a ride. When you get back to town from your ride, stop back into my saloon and I'll buy you a drink."

"No thanks Belle. I'm more interested in finding that black stallion," replied Rex. "Are you sure you don't know any more about the stallion than you told me?"

"I told you everything I know," answered Belle. "That was another reason Eddy and I came out this way for a ride. I felt very bad about Dean buying that black stallion from Oliver's stable hand the way he did when Oliver Columbo was gone. I know Dean wouldn't have bought that horse if he had known who really owned it. Now that Dean doesn't work for me, I can't help you. I am so sorry about this.

Eddie thought he knew where we could find Dean, but we didn't have any luck. If there is anything else I can help you with, just ask. I'll be glad to help anyway I can."

"I appreciate that," replied Rex. "I'm sorry I came into your saloon and behaved like I did. I was lead to believe you had all the answers to the missing stallion. I have to get that horse back now."

"I'm sorry too," replied Belle. "I wish I could help you more. As I said, I just don't know what to do to help."

"Do you have any idea where we can look?" questioned Rex. "Anything would help."

"There's a town thirty miles north of Dodge called Brownsville. I have heard rumors that Dean may be there," suggested Belle. "I would go with you but I have to get back to my saloon and go to work."

"I know where that is," stated Marshal Allen. "That would be a good days ride and back."

"Thanks for your help Belle," Rex went on to say. "Marshal Allen, lead the way."

As Rex and his squad began to ride down the road, Belle and Eddie resumed their ride to Dodge. After Belle was out of sight, Rex ordered his squad to stop.

"I don't buy Belle's story about Dean being in Brownsville. I think it's a wild goose chase," explained Rex to his men. "Stephen, take Hannibal and follow Belle," requested Rex. "The rest of us are going back to the rocky hill that Belle rode down and try to see where she came from. Maybe we'll get lucky and find your stallion."

"But I want to go with you to try and find Thunder," replied an anxious Stephen. "Can't somebody else go?"

"I understand your frustration about wanting to find your horse," answered Rex. "I feel that it's my fault that you lost your horse because I talked you into bringing your horse back in time with you. One way or another were going to find Thunder.

It would be better if you and Hannibal follow Belle. I need Marshal Allen's help because he knows the territory. Who and Because don't know the territory and I'm not going to let Scooter out of my sight. That means you and Hannibal are elected to go."

"I understand what your reasoning is," replied Stephen. "I wish this was all a dream, then I would have Thunder back with me. I'll do as you say."

"When you get to Dodge, find Columbo and tell him what's happened so far. Tell him to assign two men to watch Belle's Saloon at all times," instructed Rex. "She knows a lot more than she's telling me. I'm sure of it. Use your two way radios to keep in touch. OK, get going."

As Rex and his boys were out of Bell's sight, Belle and Eddie quickly rode toward the road to the telegraph wires that went into Twin Forks. As they approached the wires, Belle instructed Eddie to climb up the post to the wires and cut them down. Within a couple minutes the wires were cut.

"Come on Eddie, let's get back to the road to Dodge in case we run into those Marshals again," instructed Belle.

As Belle and Eddy rode out of sight of the cut wires, they saw Hannibal and Stephen trailing them.

"Look Belle, two of the Marshals are following us," observed Eddie. "I don't think they saw me cut those wires. I got those wires cut just in time."

"Let's just ride slow back to Dodge," suggested Belle. "Just as Michael would say, as long as we don't do anything out of the ordinary, they won't suspect a thing."

Chapter 41

RAIDING TWIN FORKS

Back at the hide out, the gang was preparing to leave and ride to Twin Forks. Danny was sitting on Thunder as The Stunning Kid with Michael's gang Tiny, Art, Big Bob, Charlie, The Chill and The Oklahoma Kid setting on their horses besides him.

"I want to take the precaution of having my gang ride out of the hide out first," instructed Michael. "If Marshal Allen is with any of the Marshals that followed Belle to the hide out last night, he won't know who my men are. If none of The Marshals are not in the area, the rest of us will follow. We need to ride around Dodge to get to Twin Forks."

As Michael's gang rides between the big boulders that conceal the hide out, they see The Marshals in the distance.

"Danny, you, Charlie, The Chill and The Oklahoma Kid stay back," ordered Big Bob. "Art and Tiny, you come with me. We need to circle around The Marshals and approach them from the other side."

A couple of minutes later, Big Bob, Art and Tiny was riding towards The Marshals away from the hide out entrance.

"Howdy Gents," greeted Big Bob to The Marshals. "Nice day, isn't it?"

"Howdy," replied Marshal Allen to Big Bob. "What outfit do you ride for?"

"None at this time," replied Big Bob. "Do you know anybody looking for hands?"

150

"No, I'm afraid I don't," answered Marshal Allen. "We're all Marshals and we're looking for a gang that has a big black stallion. Have you seen a big black stallion around? That horse is what we want to find."

"Have any of you seen a big black stallion?" Big Bob asked his men.

"I haven't seen a black horse." replied Art.

"Me either," answered Tiny. "You know the three of us have been together for the last week."

"I'm sorry, we can't help you," insisted Big Bob. "We're just riding through the territory looking for work."

"If you do see a black stallion, come to The Marshals Office in Dodge," Marshal Allen went on to say. "You'll get paid a good reward if we can get that stallion back."

"You bet we will. We can certainly use the money," insisted Big Bob. "Would you like us to ride with you to help find that stallion? Now that I think about it, I thought I saw a black stallion about three miles up that road yesterday."

"No thanks, we'll go check it out, replied Marshal Allen. "Come on boys. Let's ride."

"We're always glad to help the law," stated Big Bob.

After The Marshals were out of sight, Big Bob, Art and Tiny rode back to the big boulders concealing the hide out where Danny and the rest of the gang waited. Big Bob then reported to Michael about his encounter with The Marshals. Knowing The Marshals were no longer a threat to the gang, Michael took the gang to Twin Forks.

Once the gang reached Twin Forks, Dean took his gang to the Sheriff's Office where they found Sheriff Gold and two of his Deputies. Dean and his gang entered the Sheriff's Office with their faces masked and guns drawn. They ordered the lawmen to take off their guns and to get into the jail cell.

"Just who are you men and what are you doing here?" asked Sheriff Gold. "What do you want and why are you doing this to me and my Deputies?"

"We're part of The Stunning Kid's Gang and we're putting you in your own jail, compliments of The Stunning Kid," answered Dean.

"Now that your in jail, we are free to rob the bank and the store owners here in Twin Forks."

"You're not going to get away with this," yelled Sheriff Gold. "When I get out of here, I'm going to form a posse and come after you."

"Says who?" replied Ace.

"Says me," roared the Sheriff." I'm going to catch up with you one day. This is going to be the last bank you'll ever rob."

"How about I put a couple of slugs in The Sheriff, boss?" asked Ace.

"That's too noisy. That will alert the town that something isn't right," explained Dean. "If The Sheriff doesn't sit on the cot in the jail and shut up, we'll have to tie and gag him and his Deputies.

Mugs and Shorty, you stay here and keep an eye on the Sheriff. If he starts to get out of line again, it may be a better idea to do as Ace said, shoot him and his Deputies.

Lefty, you go tell Michael it's OK to send The Stunning Kid to the bank and then come back here. The three of us are going to wait for The Stunning Kid to rob the bank. Then The Stunning Kid is going to join us in robbing all the store owners after he gives the money to Michael.

Michael can then ride out of town and wait for us with the money. Michael is going to be sitting on his horse out on the street and act as our security because of his broken leg."

Five minutes later, The Stunning Kid enters The Twin Forks Bank with his guns drawn.

"OK ladies and gents, this is a hold up. Drop your guns and everybody walk over to that wall and face it with your hands up," ordered The Stunning Kid. "Don't anybody try to be a hero or you're going to be a dead hero. You there. Come with me and open up the vault."

After the gang filled their saddle bags full of money, The Stunning Kid said, "Well, the money is all here. Everybody in this bank, stay in this bank for a half hour. There are several more members of my gang outside and we're going to be busy here in town. If anybody leaves this bank before then, we will blow your head off.

Don't count on Sheriff Gold to help you. Right now, we have him in his own jail. OK men. Let's get out of here and finish what we came here to do."

The Stunning Kid and his men then rushed out of the bank and gave Michael the saddle bags full of money and then signaled Dean to bring his men to join him.

As the store owners watched the gang from their windows, they quickly locked the front doors of their stores and pulled down the shades.

"Oh, they want to play games," yelled Ace. "I was hoping they would do that. They may think that's going to keep us out of their stores. Don't they realize we're going to break down their doors and bust all of their windows?"

"Let's start with that general store," suggested Big Bob. "That store owner always has given me a tough time when I've gone into his store. He doesn't have Sheriff Gold to protect him now."

Within a couple of minutes, the door to the general store was busted open.

"Get out of my store," ordered the nervous store owner who was holding a shotgun.

Seeing the shotgun, Ace fired his forty five hitting the store owner who dropped the shotgun and fell to the floor.

The store owner's wife was watching from the doorway going to the back of the store. Seeing her husband on the floor, she rushed to him kneeling on the floor, crying. She picked up the shotgun and aimed it at Ace. Seeing this, Ace fired again hitting the woman who fell to the floor next to her husband.

Thirty minutes later, the gang mounted their horses and rode out of town, shooting in the air with their pistols to stampede all the horses in town. As the gang rode out of town, the store owners and townspeople rushed over to The Sheriff's Office.

As The Sheriff and his two Deputies were let out of jail, The Sheriff asked, "What was all the shooting about? Was the bank robbed?"

Answering The Sheriff's questions, the townspeople told The Sheriff about the raid on the town, with the bank being robbed and how it looked like a personal shoot out with the store owner and his wife being shot.

"That's just great. We can't let them get away with that. I'm going after this gang of thieves and murderers," announced Sheriff Gold. "Whoever is going with me, get your horse and be in front of my office ready to ride."

Chapter 42

COLUMBO GOES TO TWIN FORKS

Two hours later, as the stage pulled into Dodge a rider in front of the stage depot began to yell, "The stage is coming! The stage is coming!"

As the stage approached the depot, the driver started yelling for Marshal Allen saying, "Twin Forks has just been raided by Stunning Kid and his gang."

Hearing this, Columbo and his men rushed over to the stage depot.

"I hear your looking for Marshal Allen," Columbo said to the driver. "I'm Marshal Columbo. What's all the excitement about?"

"The Stunning Kid and his gang just raided Twin Forks. They robbed the bank and the store owners. The owner and his wife to the general store was wounded very badly," explained the driver. "Where is Marshal Allen?"

"The Stunning Kid, impossible," stated Colombo. "How do you get to Twin Forks and how far is it?"

"It was The Stunning Kid. Everybody in town saw him," insisted the driver. "Take the south road out of Dodge. It will take you four hours to get there."

"Did The Stunning Kid ride a black stallion?" asked Stephen.

"He not only rode a black stallion, he was dressed in black with a black mask and a Mexican Hat," replied the driver. "The Sheriff and his posse is out looking for him now. If you take that rode to Twin Forks, you just might run into him."

OK, West Side Kids, let's get back to The Marshal's Office now," ordered Columbo. "I have to contact Rex right away."

A couple minutes later, the gang was back at The Marshal's Office.

Picking up his two way radio, Columbo began to call Rex. After Columbo explained to Rex what the stagecoach driver said, Rex instructed Columbo to contact his grandfather, Oliver and ask him to keep an eye on Dodge with Stephen and Hannibal. If there was any trouble, Oliver was to call Rex on his two way radio. Columbo was then to take his squad to Twin Forks and find out about this Stunning Kid by interviewing the towns people about the raid.

"If you see The Stunning Kid and his gang, call me on the radio," instructed Rex. "Then I want you to follow him. After I join you, we can try and catch him and his gang."

Rex also instructed Columbo to contact Moe Mannix to have a doctor and nurse from the 21st century ready to be transported to the edge of Twin Forks when he arrives. The doctor and his nurse can then ride into Twin Forks in a buggy with the squad to treat the wounds of the store owner and his wife.

Four hours later, Columbo and his squad was at the edge of Twin Forks with a buggy for the doctor and nurse. Columbo then contacted Moe Mannix and told him he was ready for the doctor. A couple seconds later the doctor and nurse appeared in front of Columbo.

Now that the gang was all there, they began to ride into Twin Forks arriving at The Sheriff's Office a couple minutes later. Seeing that The Sheriff wasn't in his office, Columbo asked his squad to spread out and find out where the doctor's office was and the wounded husband and wife.

Ten minutes later Columbo, the doctor and nurse from the 21st century was in the Dr. Hoffman's Office.

"Hello doctor," greeted Columbo. "I'm Marshal Columbo and this is Dr. Genesis and his nurse Joanne who is a RN."

"What's a RN?" quizzed Dr. Hoffman?"

"RN is short for a Registered Nurse who graduated from a nursing program," explained Dr. Genesis. "A RN treats patients, provides advice and emotional support.

We understand that you have a wounded husband and wife here in your office. How are they doing?"

"They're not doing too good," answered Dr. Hoffman. "I took the bullets out and I bandaged them. There is not much more that I can do for them but wait. I think they lost too much blood, because the bullets did too much damage for me to save either one of them."

"Dr. Hoffman, would you mind if I took a look at them?" asked Dr. Genesis. "I've had a lot of experience in gunshot wounds."

"Be my guest. I think they're too far gone for you to save them," answered Dr. Hoffman. "They're in the other room."

"Come on Joanne, we've got work to do," ordered Dr. Genesis. "Dr. Hoffman, would you like to come with us and give us a hand?"

"I'll help anyway that I can, but I don't see the use," answered Dr. Hoffman.

"Joanne, first check their blood pressure, temperature and then get their blood type so we can give them the correct plasma, stat," ordered Dr. Genesis.

Dr. Hoffman, would you help Joanne while I look over their wounds. I think I'm going to have to go in and operate on their wounds."

"Yes Dr. Genesis," answered Dr. Hoffman. "Are you sure you know what you're doing? This is all new to me. I'm anxious to see what you're going to do."

"When I'm done operating on this married couple, they will be like brand new," promised Dr. Genesis.

As the doctors worked, Columbo and his crew went to the bank and the stores to ask the needed questions about the raid and robberies at Twin Forks.

Finding out what he needed to know, Columbo called Rex on the radio. Because of the distance Columbo and Rex had trouble hearing each other. Columbo then called his grandfather, Oliver because the distance was closer. He told Oliver what happened in Twin Forks and then Oliver was to call Rex and tell him about Twin Forks.

As Oliver explained to Rex about the details of the raid on Twin Forks, Rex followed with instructions about providing security for Dodge. Oliver was told to close up the banks and all the stores in Dodge and then to hire several Deputies and have them posted around Dodge in groups, because the gang was last known to be traveling towards Dodge.

Columbo and his gang then mounted their horses and started to ride back towards Dodge, looking for The Stunning Kid and Sheriff Gold on the way.

A half hour later, Columbo saw Sheriff Gold and his posse riding up the trail toward him and his men.

"Sheriff Gold!" yelled Columbo. "Over here! Can I have a word with you?"

As Sheriff Gold rode up to Columbo, Columbo asked, "Did you find any trace of The Stunning Kid and his gang?"

"Not a trace," answered Sheriff Gold. "They had to go north towards Dodge. I know they wouldn't ride very far west of Twin Forks. Can you imagine riding a week without seeing a human being or a town? Just who are you by the way?"

"I'm U. S. Marshal Columbo and these are my Deputies. We're from Dodge."

"I thought Dodge belonged to Marshal Allen," replied Sheriff Gold. "Isn't he the Marshal there anymore?"

"Yes, he certainly is. He is now a U. S. Marshal and we're all working together to round up the gang that is doing the robbing and stealing," answered Columbo.

"You mean The Stunning Kid and his gang, don't you?" asked Sheriff Gold.

"It wasn't The Stunning Kid and he doesn't have a gang," replied Columbo.

"You have it all wrong, Marshal. It was The Stunning Kid and his gang. There must have been at least fourteen or fifteen," insisted Sheriff Gold. "Everybody in Twin Forks saw him with his black stallion. You can't tell me any different."

"Sheriff, I've got news for you," explained Columbo. "All of my men know who The Stunning Kid really is. He came to Dodge to work with Marshal Allen as a Deputy Marshal to rid the town of The Dean Dickerson Gang.

Dean Dickerson was working in Belle's Saloon. Dean bought his black stallion and found The Stunning Kids outfit with the saddle from the stable hand in Dodge while The Stunning Kid was out of town. I want to get that stallion back."

"And who is the real Stunning Kid if that was somebody else who robbed the bank?" asked Sheriff Gold.

"I guess it doesn't make any difference now if you know who the real Stunning Kid is," explained Columbo. "Stephen Edwards is The Stunning Kid and a Deputy Marshal. Among us there are fourteen U. S. Marshals and U. S. Deputy Marshals. Stephen Edwards has always been one of us. Now our next problem is to capture the gent pretending to be The Stunning Kid."

"So, Stephen Edwards is the great Stunning Kid. He sure had us fooled," replied Sheriff Gold. "I just can't believe it."

"My advice to you Sheriff Gold is to hire several Deputies of your own until we capture this gang. They won't be back. They set out what they meant to do. I think we better alert all the surrounding towns to be on the alert for this gang," suggested Columbo.

"When you get back to Twin Forks would you send a telegram to these towns. For security purposes, they better all be hiring extra Deputies. If they don't have a Sheriff or Town Marshal, they better be calling for volunteers to form a vigilante committee. There is only one thing to do. Strike back and strike back hard."

"Yes, I will do that as soon as I get back to Twin Forks. I can't send a telegram to Dodge because the wires have been cut," replied Sheriff Gold. "I want this gang and I want them bad. I have personal reasons for catching that gang. They locked me in my own jail. Nobody does that to me and gets away with it."

"Don't worry about Dodge, we already sent them a smoke signal. They are already prepared for the gang if they come to Dodge," answered Columbo. "We're all going to have to unite and as a friend of mine said, we need to have a Paul Revere to capture this gang."

"A Paul Revere. What's a Paul Revere?" asked Sheriff Gold. "I don't know any Paul Revere."

"You know, Paul Revere and The Raiders from The Revolutionary War. Paul was The Midnight Cowboy of 1776," explained Columbo. "He rode around yelling; The British are coming. The British are coming."

"Just who is this Paul Revere and The Raiders? They better not come to raid Twin Forks like The Stunning Kid and his gang, because we're going to be ready for them. What's this about Scooter and smoke signals? Just what are you talking about?" asked Sheriff Gold.

"Forget it, Sheriff Gold. I was just mumbling about Paul Revere and The Raiders," answered Columbo. "Don't worry about them. This is the name of a group that entertains people with their singing and playing their instruments. They aren't going to raid Twin Forks.

I don't believe it. I'm starting to talk like Scooter, and you wouldn't understand," explained Columbo as the men in his squad laughed out loud.

Chapter 43

THE GANG IS COMING HOME

Back in Dodge, Eddie reported to Belle that there was only two Marshals left in town. They were Stephen and Hannibal.

"I know the gang is coming home from their raid on Twin Forks," replied Belle to Eddie. "Now would be a good time for the gang to raid Dodge just as they did on Twin Forks. Ride out and find Michael and let him know what I think."

Fifteen minutes later Eddie found the gang and gave Michael and the gang the message from Bell.

"We're in luck. That's good information to know," explained Michael to the gang. "There is only two Marshals in Dodge and they won't be expecting us. We might as well stop in Dodge and pick up some bonus cash on the way to the hide out. We already have a good strategy that is working for us. Let's go to Dodge for the execution. Today is really going to pay off with another raid. We've got to move fast and hit hard before the rest of the Marshals come back."

Ten minutes later the gang was on the edge of Dodge.

"Dean, you take your men into Dodge and go to The Marshal's Office," ordered Michael. "You know what to do."

"This is my personal party and I'm going to enjoy this," roared Ace. "Stephen Edwards won't be expecting to see me so soon. Now I'm going to be able to pay this tough Stephen Edwards back for what he did to me. I'm going to talk to him alone and have some fun with him. Then it will be my pleasure to be putting him in his bird cage."

"Take it easy. You just do your job or you're going to have to stay here," ordered Michael. "I don't want any slip ups or have to put up with any failures. I don't know what this Stephen Edwards did to you. But I guarantee it will be a picnic compared to what I'm going to do to you if you don't tend to business."

"All right, I will get the job done for you," promised a nervous Ace.

"See that you do. I don't like to say things twice!" shouted Michael. "OK, this is it boys. Here we go again. Dean, It's time to ride out of here. Move out."

As Stephen was looking out the window of The Marshal's Office, up rode The Masked Dean Dickerson gang.

"We've got trouble," Stephen said to Hannibal and Oliver. "There are several masked men outside. Hannibal grab your AR15 rifle. Oliver get your 12 gauge shotgun."

As Ace opened the door, there was two AR15 rifles and a shotgun pointed at him. Ace immediately shut the door yelling, "Alright men, clear out of town. It's a trap." as he ran to his horse.

Stephen and Hannibal followed running outside firing their AR rifles as the gang rode away. Riding up to Michael, Ace yelled for the gang to ride to the hide out, because there must have been thirty men in The Marshal's Office.

As the gang rode away, Oliver called Rex on his two way radio about the gang's visit to Dodge. Rex replied that he was too far away from Dodge to help. He was on his way back to Dodge and should be there in an hour.

Chapter 44

It's Grubstake

On the way back to the hide out, a man was seen riding his horse down the road with his pack mule.

"It's Grubstake," boomed Ace. "After him."

As the gang began racing down the road, Grubstake urged his horse and mule to go faster. After a short chase, Grubstake was surrounded by the gang.

"Now we have you Grubstake and there is no Stunning Kid around to save you," yelled Ace. "This time you're going to tell me where your gold mine is or else."

"Like I told you before, I'm not going to tell you where my gold mine is, not to you or anybody else," answered Grubstake.

"Let's take him to the hide out," ordered Michael. "He'll talk after we get him there."

"Let's go Grubstake," demanded Ace as he pulled out his revolver.

Now the gang is back at the hide out and Grubstake is tied to a chair.

"Grubstake, I'm Michael, The Magnificent. Have you ever heard of me?"

"Yes, I heard of you. Who hasn't?" answered Grubstake. "Now I suppose you're going to tell me what you're going to do to me if I don't tell you where the mine is. Well I'm not telling you or Ace or anybody else."

"Suits me. Have it your way," reasoned Michael. "I think after you've gone a few days without food and water, that will loosen your tongue."

"Come on Michael. Forget Grubstake and start counting the money from our last raid," insisted Dean. "Grubstake isn't going anywhere."

"OK Dean, I'll start counting the money. I'm as anxious to see what we made from our raid on Twin Forks as everyone else," laughed Michael.

As Michael sat down at the table with all the bags of money in front of him, he began counting the money from The Twin Forks raid dividing the money up in shares to pay the gang off from the raid. Drinks are poured and a celebration begins. A couple hours later, Michael calls everybody together for another planned raid.

"Congratulations boys. After what we did at Twin Forks, nobody is going to trust The Stunning Kid anymore. I think if The Stunning Kid disappears for a while it will keep the law busy looking for him," explained Michael. "I think it's time for Indians to start raiding the settlers and rustling the rancher's cattle.

I have a friend by the name of Big Jim Brady who runs a trading post for the Indians. His trading post is located in the village of Bearcat just ten miles west of Brownsville. He knows more about Indians than anybody else in the territory.

Twenty men work for Big Jim and they're for hire. If we worked with Big Jim and his men, we would make a decent tribe of Indians.

Black Eagle is the chief of the tribe. It would be bad for Black Eagle if we did the raiding as Indians because he would get the blame."

"You sure have a head on your shoulders Michael," reasoned Lefty. "We pull the jobs and make the money while somebody else gets the blame. Your going to make more money for us than Belle could ever make possible."

"I'm very much in agreement with Lefty," beamed Ace. "We're in the money now."

"I really like how you're planning the jobs," added Dean. "After Belle gets her share from our last job, she won't have any more regrets with you taking over the gang."

"Thank you, men, for the compliments," replied Michael. "Like I said from the beginning, it's just strategy and execution. How would everybody feel if we rode up to Brownsville tomorrow?" asked Michael.

"And do what?" asked Ace. "That's going to be another long ride."

"Would it be worth the ride if I said, we're all going to stay in Brownsville for a couple of days. With your newfound wealth, you can drink, you can gamble and have the time of your lives," explained Michael. "While your all enjoying yourselves, I'm going to ride over to Bearcat and have a talk with Big Jim about being Indians."

"You're always thinking Michael," laughed Dean. "What are we going to do with Belle's share of the money?"

"If it's OK with you Michael, I'll ride into Dodge and give it to her," requested Danny. "I would just like to take a break from everything and go to the hotel and rest."

"That's OK with me Danny," replied Michael. "That sounds like a good idea. You can watch the movements of The Marshals wasting their time looking for The Stunning Kid while your there.

The best part of it all is that The Stunning Kid will be right under their nose's and they won't suspect a thing. If there is something I need to know, you can send me a telegram at Brownsville.

With the way you did your job as The Stunning Kid, you more than earned it. You can leave for Dodge the first thing in the morning. Just make sure your back at the hide out in four days."

Chapter 45

THE HOMESTEADER'S MEETING

Later that day, Michael and his gang was in Brownsville. Rex, Columbo, Stephen, Hannibal, Scooter and The West Side Kids was at Mr. Wilson's Homestead with Marshal Allen. A meeting was being held with ranchers and other homesteaders about fighting Dean Dickerson and his gang.

Mr. Wilson began the meeting by welcoming all the ranchers, homesteaders, The Marshal, and his men.

"I'm calling this meeting to order. We know why we're all here," Mr. Wilson began to say. "A friend of mine known as The Stunning Kid said that this is no country a man comes to for his health."

"Wait," broke in a rancher by the name of Dusty. "What do you mean The Stunning Kid is a friend of yours? He's an outlaw. A couple of days ago, him and his gang robbed a stage and then the day after that raided Twin Forks, robbing, and shooting people."

"I don't believe it. The Stunning Kid helps people and he works alone," corrected Mr. Wilson. "I meant him, and I happen to know he wouldn't do that."

"I'm Marshal Tarillo and he's right. The Stunning Kid did rob a stage and raid Twin Forks with his gang," answered Rex. "Me and my men just came to Dodge a few days ago to stop The Dean Dickerson gang. Once we can prove they're the ones behind all this violence, they will be arrested. Now with The Stunning Kid robbing and stealing, we have two gangs to deal with.

There is so much territory to cover and so many men to catch, we need to band together to stop these lawbreakers. I am going to talk to Sheriff Gold in Twin Forks and take charge of this whole operation."

"You can count me out Rex or Marshal Tarillo," announced Stephen. "I was assigned by you to come to the territory to be Marshal Allen's Deputy with Hannibal and Scooter. I've asked you for some help. Not for you to take over my job. Why don't you tell everybody the whole story of The Stunning Kid? If you don't I will."

"Stephen, calm down. You're going to spoil everything," ordered Rex.

"Everything is already spoiled for me. I just don't care anymore if everybody knows," replied Stephen. "Now if I can have everybody's attention. I am going to tell you the rest of the story of The Stunning Kid.

Rex had me come to Dodge with the purpose of being a Deputy Marshal to help Marshal Allen. Marshal Allen knows what the other purpose was. To clean up Dodge of The Dean Dickerson Gang.

My dual role was for me to be The Stunning Kid. I was doing pretty good as The Stunning Kid. Then I found out that The Dean Dickerson Gang was starting to get too big for me to handle. I went out of town with Marshal Allen to ask Rex for help. Rex decided to come to Dodge with several U. S. Deputy Marshals.

When we all came to Dodge, I went to Oliver Columbo's Stable. Something very important to me was missing. My black stallion, Thunder. The stable hand sold him to Dean Dickerson for $75.00 with my saddle and the outfit that made me The Stunning Kid. Whoever ended up with my outfit is doing the raiding and the robbing. Rex has been trying to help me get Thunder back and has no luck finding him.

Rex is responsible for loosing something very important to me and because of that I am going to give my Palomino back to Oliver. You know what I'm talking about. I don't want to be The Stunning Kid anymore or a Deputy Marshal. I just want my horse, Thunder back. Rex, here is your badge and gun you gave me. I quite!"

"But Stephen, I came to Dodge to help you," explained an anxious Scooter. "You and Hannibal are my best friends. I'm going with you. If you quit, I quit."

"Get away from me you idiot. You're always doing something stupid and I want you to stay away from me," ordered Stephen. "I don't want any more to do with any of you."

"Stephen, what's wrong with you? Scooter has always looked up to you as a good friend. You or nobody else talks to Scooter the way you just did and gets away with it," replied an angry Hannibal as he raised his fist to hit Stephen. "Scooter would do anything for you, and you treat him like this."

Hannibal then took a swing at Stephen with his right hand and missed. Stephen then punched Hannibal, knocking him on the floor.

OK big man. we'll stay clean out of your life," promised Hannibal as he lay-ed on the floor looking up at Stephen. "Don't you ever speak to Scooter or me again or I'm going to come looking for you with my 9mm pistol."

Standing there staring at Hannibal, with a sad look on his face, Stephen immediately went out the door slamming it and he climbed up on his Palomino for the last time. He then rode away to Oliver's stables to give him back his horse and to get his horse Lightning.

"I knew it. I just knew The Stunning Kid wasn't behind the robberies and the raids," boomed Mr. Wilson. "That young man has tried to help all of us and in the process, he lost something special to him. That horse meant the world to him. I know we want to fight The Dean Dickerson Gang, but I think our first priority is to get that young man's stallion back to him."

"I agree," roared Dusty. "Just to sit here and listen to his story and to see him leave that way makes me feel so bad for him. I'm going to try and find his stallion. Is everybody with me?"

"We sure are," yelled everybody.

"First of all," added Uncle Columbo. "Hannibal, Scooter, I want you to know that Stephen didn't really mean what he said to you. Just keep your distance. Give him some time to himself. The job he was trying to do must really have gotten to him. It was the last straw when he lost Thunder and we haven't any idea how to find him.

When he comes to his senses, I want both of you to give me your word that you will still be the best of friends."

"OK Uncle Columbo, I promise we'll still be friends," answered Hannibal.

"What about you Scooter?" asked Uncle Columbo.

"I'll always be Stephen's friend," replied Scooter. "I know he didn't mean what he said to me. I came to Dodge to be his Tonto. He'll always be The Lone Ranger to me."

"What do you mean he'll be The Lone Ranger?" asked Mr. Wilson. "Just who is The Lone Ranger? Who is Tonto?"

"I'll tell you who The Lone Ranger is," explained Marshal Allen. "He's a make believe character who wears a mask like The Stunning Kid, only his mask covers around the eyes and nose. He uses silver bullets and rides a white horse called Silver. Tonto is an Indian who is his side kick and rides a paint called Scout.

They ride all over the west to bring justice to everybody they meet. They help the weak or the victims of lawbreakers and never want a reward or get paid for what they do. Their intent is to the catch criminals and put them in jail. When their job is done, they never stay for the thank you. They immediately leave for their next job riding out of town with Tonto, The Lone Ranger yells, Hi Ho Silver and Away."

"We sure could use somebody like that now." reasoned Mr. Wilson. "I bet he could find that black stallion."

"We do have somebody like that, Stephen," Rex informed everyone. "If we can find that black stallion, I'm sure we'll find the gang. If we band together, we can all be The Lone Ranger and Tonto for Stephen if we can get his stallion back."

Chapter 46

MEETING BIG JIM

After reaching Brownsville, Michael's men, found rooms at the hotel. Michael continued his ride to Bearcat to meet his friend Big Jim Brady as his men settled in Brownsville. They all went to the bath house to take baths, put on clean clothes, and went to the barber for a shave and haircut, preparing for their first night of fun.

Just as Michael rode into Bearcat, he saw Big Jim's Trading Post. A couple minutes later, Michael was inside.

Seeing Big Jim, Michael said, "Hello you old Bearcat. How have you been?"

"I'm doing great as usual you old horse thief," answered Big Jim. "I'm making some good money from these Indians."

"You mean your practically stealing from these Indians," replied Michael

"I wouldn't do that," insisted Big Jim. "I'm an honest merchant and I always give these Indians a good price on everything."

"I'm sure you do because your halo is showing. Everybody who believes that should stand on their head," laughed Michael. "How would you and your boys like to be partners with me and my boys stealing cattle the honest way?"

"I sure would. There's a rancher by the name of Bill Elliot who has a ranch a couple miles from here. He is always coming into the trading post giving me trouble," explained Big Jim. "I'm sure he wouldn't mind paying me for that trouble with his cattle. Who have you and your gang been collecting from?"

Michael then went on to explain to big Jim about working with The Dean Dickerson Gang and The Stunning Kid. The next thing he told Big Jim was about the new Marshals in Dodge City and how he intends to avoid contacting them.

"With the lawmen looking for The Stunning Kid, he is going to have to disappear for now," Michael went on to say. "I always like to watch my step and my next step is Indians. My gang is going to be Indians. That's where you come in."

"You want me to use my Indians to rustle cattle?" asked Big Jim.

"No, it's better than that," replied Michael. "I want your men to work with my men and we will all be The Indians.

We'll rustle the cattle and The Indians will get blamed for it. We'll be Indians while the law is looking for The Stunning Kid and Black Eagle's Tribe. No going to the hide out or running from the law. Instead we'll be having a good time spending our money out in the open while the law is looking for Indians and The Stunning Kid."

"That's very clever. You have a good head on your shoulders," reasoned Big Jim,

"Thanks, Big Jim. It seems like I've heard that before," beamed Michael. "A long time ago I learned about strategy and execution from my father. I have followed his advice and have been very successful in using this. It has really paid off."

"How many men do you have?" asked Big Jim. "I have twenty men."

"There is fourteen of us plus Belle, who owns Belle's Saloon in Dodge," answered Michael.

"I've heard of Belle. How did you get tangled up with her?" asked Big Jim.

"It's a long story," answered Michael. "She hired me to get rid of The Stunning Kid because he was trying to take over her territory. The Stunning Kid saved my life when he found me along the roadside with a broken leg. I was in debt to Belle and The Stunning Kid.

Belle made me keep the deal with her to get rid of The Stunning Kid. Now Belle's gang is mine. I decided to have one of the gang members impersonate The Stunning Kid to rob and steel instead of killing the real Stunning Kid. This way The Stunning Kid would have a bad reputation, and nobody would trust him. That was the only way I knew how to pay off both of my debts."

"I'll tell you what I'll do," offered Big Jim. "Because I have the Trading Post for the Indians, I'll can supply any Indian gear you need for the raids and my twenty men for sixty per cent of the profits."

"This was my idea. How about giving me at least forty five per cent?" asked Michael.

"This may be your idea of strategy, but you won't have a very good execution without me and my men," answered Big Jim. "I get sixty per cent and that is my final offer. Besides, I know a cattle buyer who will buy the cattle without asking any questions."

"That's a deal," promised Michael as he put his hand out to shake with Big Jim's hand. "You don't know it, but I would have accepted less."

"I think we made a fair deal. You're my friend and I wouldn't cheat you," promised Big Jim. "I hope you remember this in the future. I would like to start by rustling the cattle from the rancher I was telling you about. How long before you can get your men here?"

"Right now, twelve of my men are in Brownsville. I gave them three days in Brownsville to drink, play cards and have a good time," replied Michael. "That will give us three days to ride out to Bill Elliot's ranch to plan our strategy and to get the Indian gear together."

"This is going to fit into my plans just beautiful," admitted Big Jim. "I have been trying to figure out how to start an Indian War. If you follow the road out of the other side of Bearcat, it will lead you to The Black Fork Road. Then you take the left fork and it will take you to Black Water Canyon where Black Eagle's Tribe is.

Because I want that land, I have already sold Black Eagle 100 repeating rifles. If I can start an all-out Indian War, that will bring the cavalry. The Indians will be forced to leave their land and I will take over their land. I have already planned to do some cattle rustling, and this would be a perfect place to hide the stolen cattle."

"When I came into your Trading Post, you called me an Old Horse Thief," laughed Michael. "It's beginning to look like we're both Old

Cattle Thief's. I think if we became partners a long time ago, the whole territory would all belong to us by now."

"After we rustle Bill Elliot's cattle, it will be a start," replied Big Jim. "What do you say we ride to his ranch where you and I can begin planning our strategy now."

"The sooner the better," answered Michael. "I'm ready to ride."

Chapter 47

DANNY AND BELLE

Belle is now sitting at her desk in her office at the saloon. There is a knock on the door and the door opens and Danny enters Belle's Office.

"Hi Danny," greeted Belle. "Are you starting to be yourself now that you have some time to play cards and relax?"

"I'm feeling just fine," answered Danny. "I don't know if you noticed, but that tough Deputy Stephen Edwards is a different story. He is no longer a Deputy Marshal. He has been playing cards here in the saloon for a couple of days now. His clothes are filthy. He's unshaven and drunk."

"Has he said anything to you as to why he's not a Deputy Marshal anymore?" asked Belle.

"Since he's been drunk, you can't shut him up," replied Danny. "What I've been able to find out is that he got really mad at Marshal Tarillo at a Homesteader's Meeting about fighting our gang. He gave The Marshal back his gun and badge. Before he left, he punched his best friend Hannibal to the floor and told Scooter he was stupid."

"Did you find out what made Stephen do that?" asked Belle.

"I sure did. This is the part you're really going to like," explained Danny. "You hired Michael to get rid of The Stunning Kid. Michael got the job done alright. It turns out that Stephen Edwards is or was The Stunning Kid. All it took to get rid of The Stunning Kid was for Dean Dickerson to buy his black stallion from under him.

Stephen became so depressed because he lost his stallion that he has completely fallen to pieces. Stephen has become such a mess that I even feel sorry for him. If he keeps this up, he's going to replace Marshal Allen as the town drunk. Right now, Stephen is downstairs drinking and playing cards."

"If what you're telling me is true, this is opportunity knocking at the door," exclaimed Belle. "I said I wanted The Stunning Kid working for me and now it may happen."

"That would be fine with me if Stephen Edwards worked as The Stunning Kid in my place," reasoned Danny. "I just never felt the part and was very uncomfortable being The Stunning Kid."

"Danny, I have always liked you because of your personality," admitted Belle. "You have always been my favorite member of the gang. You are really a nice person for being a bad man."

"Thanks for what you just said," beamed Danny. "I never planned on being in a gang. I was broke and that's when Dean Dickerson talked me into joining his gang.

I've always wanted to be a cattle rancher. When I get my money saved from the jobs we are going to pull, I am going to buy a ranch far away from Dodge. When I do, I would be very happy if you lived on my ranch with me."

"That sounds very inviting to me," reasoned Belle. "Michael took over my gang and I am tired of living and working in this saloon. Help me get Stephen Edwards to join our gang.

Dean's been wanting to but my saloon. If we can make some more money with the gang and Dean buys the saloon, then I will go with you and leave Dodge forever. If we can go somewhere that nobody knows us, we can be one of those respectable people. I think I would like that very much.

Danny, I think it's time that we started to work as a team to get that ranch. Would you go back downstairs and work on Stephen Edwards to see what else you can find out and get him to trust you. If it begins to sound like he can be talked into joining our gang, tell him that you might be able to help him get his horse back. Once you get him roped in, send him up to my office.

When Michael contacts me in a couple of days, I will tell him about Stephen Edwards. He meant Stephen as The Stunning Kid. Since he is so smart with his strategy and execution, he should know what to do about Stephen."

"Yes Belle, it sounds like my dreams of getting a ranch is going to come true," replied Danny. "I've always cared about you, but I never thought I would have a chance with you. Now I can stop worrying, because I am not only am I going to get a ranch, now I'm going to have somebody to share it with and it's going to be you."

Chapter 48

I Can Fix Your Problem

An hour later, Stephen began to stumble up the steps to Belle's Office. As he reached the door to Belle's Office, he knocked on the door.

"Come in Stephen" requested Belle.

"Hello Belle," replied Stephen. "Can I sit down? I don't feel so good."

"You don't look very good. Sit in that chair in front of my desk," replied Belle. "Danny has been telling me that you have been going through some bad times. He asked me to help you. He wants to be your friend and he is very worried about you."

"Nobody can help me, nobody," reasoned Stephen.

"Stephen, remember when you rescued me from my runaway horse? You saved my life and I still owe you," promised Belle. "Tell me what I can do to fix your problem and I will do that for you. If you keep up your drinking, you're going to be the town drunk like Marshal Allen was. I don't want that to happen to you."

"You think you can really help me. Nah, you can't help me. Impossible, ridiculous, nobody can," objected Stephen. "You can't help me, and you don't owe me for saving your life. I just happened to be there when your horse ran away with you. I would have done that for anybody.

If that is all you wanted, I'm going back to my poker game. That may be a good idea to be the town drunk. It will be like going to The

Funny Farm. That way I don't have to deal with my problem, because life will be beautiful all the time."

"Please don't leave, Stephen. Danny told me what is bothering you and I can help," explained Belle. "I'll come right out with it. You saved me from a runaway horse. Now I'm going to save you from a disappearing horse.

Someone bought your black stallion and it's disappeared, and you want him back. I can get him back for you if you agree to certain conditions. If it were up to me, there would be no conditions. It isn't up to me."

"I thought you told Marshal Tarillo you didn't know anything about what happened to my stallion," explained Stephen. "I don't even want to mention that man's name because I can't stand him anymore. It's his fault my stallion is gone and it's not like he even cares.

Someday I'm going to get even with him. Nothing would give me more pleasure than to point my forty five right at his face and shoot him between the eyes."

"Really," replied Belle. "I can't stand Marshal Tarillo either. What would you say if I told you that I can help you get even with The Marshal and get your stallion back?"

"And just how are you going to do that? Do you have a magic wand or something?" asked Stephen.

"I'm sure you know that Dean Dickerson bought your stallion from the stable hand along with your outfit as The Stunning Kid," explained Belle. "How would you like to ride again as The Stunning Kid on your black stallion and get paid some big money? Think about it. This can also be your chance to get even with Marshal Tarillo."

"You bet I would," roared Stephen. "You tell me the terms and you've got a Stunning Kid. By the way, who was The Stunning Kid after you got my stallion and belongings?"

"It was Danny," answered Belle. "For your information, Danny did not like being The Stunning Kid. Michael gave him that job and he hated what he did, because he is too nice of a person."

"We have a new boss of our gang known as Michael, The Magnificent. He told us how you saved his life when you found him along side of the road with a broken leg. I hired him to go after you because of the trouble you gave my gang.

When he came to the saloon to meet with all of us, that is when I told him that his job was to stop you from interfering with my gang. Michael told me that he didn't want that job, because he owed you for saving his life. Please don't be mad at him. I made him stick to the deal he made with me.

Now he has brought his gang to town and taken over mine. It seems that you have gone around saving the lives of strangers, while I really messed up you, Michael, and me. I'm very sorry what I have done to you. If I could do it all over different, I would. Now I have to mess you up again for you to get your stallion back."

"I really don't want to be the town drunk or go to The Funny Farm. I just want to get even with Marshal Tarillo and get my stallion back. Then life will be beautiful all of the time.

He took over my job just like Michael took over your job. I guess now that I think of it, that's another good reason to be riding as The Stunning Kid for your gang," reasoned Stephen.

"I always liked the idea of being a Deputy Marshal and ridding the territory of the bad guys. Now I'm going to be one of the bad guys and another problem for Marshal Tarillo."

"Now that you're joining our gang and Michael, The Magnificent is the big boss, Marshal Tarillo doesn't have a chance to stop us. Michael will be relieved that your joining our gang and he doesn't have to hurt you."

"What about Dean Dickerson, Ace and the rest of your gang?" asked Stephen. "They don't like me because of what I did to them."

"I always admired you because you're a real man. I just couldn't believe how one man could stop a gang of eight from robbing a stage among other things," reckoned Belle.

"I don't blame them for not liking me, but I was doing my job," replied Stephen.

"You don't have anything to worry about. Danny likes you. Michael likes you and he will take care of Dean Dickerson and the rest of the boys," replied Belle. "According to Michael, he can do anything because he uses strategy and execution. With you joining our gang, we will be unstoppable."

Chapter 49
Let's Rustle Bill Elliot's Cattle

It was now the end of the third day that Michael's men's time in Brownsville was coming to a halt. It is now 6:00 p. m. and Michael has his men sitting in front of him outside at the edge of town.

"Men," Michael began to say, "I just spent three days talking to Big Jim about working with us on a couple jobs. On our next job, we are going to band together and rustle the cattle that belong to Bill Elliot. This rancher has been giving Big Jim a lot of problems, so we decided we were going to rustle his cattle as our first job."

"Are we going to be Indians like you said?" asked Ace.

"That's a good question Ace," replied Michael. "Yes, we are all going to be Indians. Big Jim has the Indian gear we need and twenty men.

With his men and us, that will make us look like a big tribe of Indians. When we ride, we have to look like we're real Indians doing the raiding and the rustling. There will be so many of us that nobody will dare to stop us."

"What's our take from this rustling?" questioned Dean.

"Since Big Jim has more men than us and is supplying the Indian gear we need, he gets sixty per cent and we get forty per cent," answered Michael.

"Is forty per cent a lot?" mumbled Lefty. "I don't know. I never went to school."

"Forty per cent is a lot," replied Michael. "We're going to do a lot of rustling while we're here in Brownsville. You will have more money in your pocket than you've ever seen before."

"Will Belle and Danny get paid since they're not helping with the rustling?" asked Shorty.

"Of course, they will get paid. They're part of the gang and they're keeping an eye on The Marshals in Dodge for us," reasoned Michael. "They may not be helping with the rustling, but they're doing this other job I gave them to do."

"When are we leaving for Big Jim's Trading Post?" inquired Mugs.

"Be saddled up and ready to go at 7:00 a. m. tomorrow morning," answered Michael.

"Big Jim and I also have another reason for the cattle rustling in this area of Brownsville. When you take the road from the other side of Bearcat, it leads to The Black Fork Road where you take the left fork and it will go to The Black Water Canyon. That is where Black Eagle's Tribe is located.

Big Jim wants Black Eagle's land, because that would be a good place to hide the stolen cattle. That is why he likes the idea of rustling cattle as Indians. He wants the Indians to get all the blame for the rustling to start an Indian War.

Black Eagle's Tribe will get blamed for the rustling. After that happens, we're going to be masked bandit's with Big Jim's men and raid Black Eagle's Village. That ought to get those red skins riled up and they will fight. The cavalry will come and run them off their land. When the Indians are gone, Big Jim will take over their land.

OK men let's get back to the saloon. Watch your drinking. I don't want anybody with hangovers riding out with us tomorrow. Is that understood?"

Five minutes later as the gang was walking into the saloon, a man from the telegraph office was walking down the boardwalk yelling, "Telegram for Michael, The Magnificent. Telegram for Michael, The Magnificent."

"Over here!" yelled Michael.

As the man was handing Michael the telegram, Michael paid him and then walked into the saloon, sat down at a table to read the telegram.

The telegram read, "Michael, The Magnificent, stop. Stephen Edwards has agreed to take Danny's place in exchange for stallion, stop. What are your orders? Stop," signed Belle.

Michael then called Dean over to his table and showed Dean the telegram.

"What do you make of the telegram?" asked Michael.

"It's got to be true or Belle wouldn't have even told Stephen about the black stallion," replied Dean. "Something happened where Belle was able to make a deal with Stephen Edwards to ride for us. It looks like we have a new member to our gang. What do you want to do about Stephen?"

"I am in debt to Stephen for saving my life," reasoned Michael. "What would you think if I sent Belle a telegram back instructing her to have Danny take Stephen to the hide out and have Danny give him his stallion to ride to Brownsville?"

"You know Belle. If Belle thinks it's a good idea, then I would say have her do it," insisted Dean.

"OK, I'll send Belle that answer. Pass this telegram around to the rest of the gang," ordered Michael. "I'm going to the telegraph office right now."

Chapter 50

STEPHEN JOINS THE GANG

It is now 7:00 p. m. in Dodge City. A man from the telegraph office is in the saloon looking for Belle to give her a telegram sent by Michael. Danny yells at the man with the telegram and says, "Over here! Belle is in her office. I'll take the telegram to her."

A couple minutes later Danny is knocking on the door to Belle's Office.

"Come on in Danny," instructed Belle. "Do you have something to tell me?"

"I have a telegram for you," replied Danny. "It's from Michael."

"Good," replied Belle. "Stay here while I read it."

Belle then read the telegram out loud to Danny, "Belle, stop. Have Danny take Edwards to the hide out, stop. Give Edwards the black stallion and the rest of his gear, stop. Send Edwards to Brownsville to get a room at the hotel, stop. Tell Edwards to wait for me at the saloon, stop." signed Michael.

"Should I take Edwards to the hide out tonight?" asked Danny.

"No, take him the first thing in the morning," answered Belle. "I never thought I was ever going to get out of this saloon. Now it looks like we're going to have our cattle ranch."

"I always thought the cattle ranch was nothing but a dream. I never really wanted to be or even liked being a badman," said an excited Danny. "Now it really looks like that dream of getting a cattle ranch is going to come true."

"You better get back downstairs and tell Stephen about going to the hide out tomorrow," explained Belle. "Don't tell Stephen any more than you have to. Remember, he used to be a Deputy Marshal. Get to know Stephen more and make sure you can trust him. When you get to the hide out, just do only what the telegram says to do."

"OK Belle, I'll do as you say. You're the boss," insisted Danny.

"When we get our cattle ranch, I hope to be more to you than just the boss," replied Belle. "Go tell Stephen the news."

A couple minutes later, Danny was sitting at the table with Stephen in the corner of the saloon.

"Do you still want to get your black stallion back?" asked Danny.

"You already know I do," reasoned Stephen. "Why do you have to ask me that again?"

"I just want to make sure you are really serious about going through the deal with Belle to get your horse back," explained Danny. "You used to be a Deputy Marshal. How do I know I can trust you?"

"Sure, I used to be a Deputy Marshal. I used to be a lot of things," answered Stephen. "You're a bad man. I'm sure you used to be a lot of things. How do I know I can trust you? How do I know I can trust Belle or your gang after what I did to them?

All I know is I want Thunder back. I raised him from a colt. If this is a trap and I don't get Thunder back, I just don't care. If your gang is going to do me in, I guess it's better than being the town drunk."

"That's all I want to know. You're going to get your horse back and nobody is going to do you in," replied Danny. "If that's how you really feel, then Belle wants me to take you to your horse tomorrow. You may be gone from Dodge between a week or a few days. That's Michael's call. Be saddled up and be ready to leave Dodge at 8:00 a. m. tomorrow morning."

"If that's all, how about you and me getting another beer and joining those boys at that other table who is playing poker?" suggested Stephen.

"No, you go ahead," offered Danny. "I just don't feel like playing cards right now. I'll see you in the morning."

Chapter 51

Stephen Gets Thunder Back

It is now 8:00 a. am the next morning. Steven has Lightning saddled up and is in front of Belle's Saloon waiting for Danny.

"Hello Stephen," greeted Danny as he rode up to Belle's Saloon. "Are you ready to go?"

"You bet I'm ready," replied Stephen. "I've been counting the minutes to finally getting Thunder back."

"Why is it so important to you to get Thunder back when you already have a nice horse," asked Danny. "I really like the white stallion you're sitting on. What's his name?"

"The horse I'm on, I named Lightning," answered Stephen. "Both of my horses are very important to me. I bought them both from the same person and raised them both from colts. I love both of my horses and they are both a big part of me. If I lost Lightning instead of Thunder, I would feel the same way."

"You are really a very lucky person Stephen. I never really felt that way about anybody or anything," exclaimed Danny. "I don't even like being a badman. The only reason I joined The Dean Dickerson Gang was because I was broke and hungry. When that happens, you'll do anything so you can be eating steady. My dream is to someday have a cattle ranch of my own. Come on. Let's go get your horse."

A half hour later, Danny and Stephen is riding between the two huge boulders that lead to the gang's hide out. As they approach the hide out, Stephen sees the corral next to the cabin. In the corral is Thunder.

"Thunder," yelled Stephen as he rode Lightning up to the corral. "It's me Stephen and Lightning. The three of us are back together again."

Stephen immediately jumped off of Lightning and ran into the corral with his arms stretched out to put around Thunder's neck.

Watching Stephen, Danny just sat on his horse as he beamed and said to Stephen, "You really did miss your stallion and I see Thunder missed you. When I rode him as The Stunning Kid, he just didn't seem to have any spirit. Now that your here, he is a very different horse.

Come on. We need to go in the cabin next. Before we do, I need to tell you what we have in the cabin. About four days ago, Michael and the gang captured Grubstake. You remember Grubstake. He was the old prospector that came into Belle's Saloon and announced that he had a gold strike. Ace wanted the location of his mine and you as The Stunning Kid rescued Grubstake from Ace.

When Michael and the gang raided Twin Forks and then was returning to the hide out, they saw Grubstake on the trail in front of them. They captured Grubstake and brought him to the hide out, because he wouldn't tell them where his mine was at. He's been sitting in the cabin tied up without food and water for the last four days.

When you go into the cabin, don't talk to Grubstake. Just pick up all you're gear that makes you The Stunning Kid, saddle up Thunder and ride out. You are to ride north to Brownsville where you will meet Michael and the gang. Get a room at the hotel and then wait at the saloon. Michael will find you."

"How far is it to Brownsville?" inquired Stephen.

"I don't know how far it is from the hide out. All I know it's thirty miles from Dodge," answered Danny. "OK, go get your gear so you can leave. I just want to finish my job so I can go back to Dodge."

"Who's going to take care of Lightning while I'm gone?" asked Stephen. "What about Grubstake? If Grubstake has been in the cabin without food and water for four days, he's not going to last much longer, and nobody will find out where his mine is."

"I can't do anything for Grubstake. Eddie who is one of the bartenders at Belle's Saloon will come out twice a day to take care of Lightning and check on Grubstake," answered Danny. "That reminds me, if I get word back that you're pulling a double cross, I will come back out to the hide out and shoot Lightning. Is that understood?"

"If it's my fault, your fault or anybody's fault, if you shoot Lightning, I will find you and I will shoot you between the eyes and you will never, ever get a cattle ranch. You better see that Lightning is well taken care of. Is that understood?" screamed Stephen.

"I understand. I'm just following orders from Belle," replied a nervous Danny. "Lightning is a beautiful horse. Orders or no orders, I couldn't really shoot him. I was just telling you what I was told to tell you."

"I know Danny. You're too nice of a person to do anything like that," reasoned Stephen. "I just couldn't take it if something was to happen to Lightning."

"Stephen, Don't worry about Lightning," insisted Danny. "I'm your friend. If I don't follow orders, Belle won't shoot me between the eyes, but Michael will. I'm tired of being a badman. All I want is my cattle ranch."

"I know just how you feel," replied Stephen. "I never intended on being a badman either. If I want to get Thunder back, I don't have any choice."

Fifteen minutes later, Stephen had Thunder saddled with his saddle bags filled with his gear to be The Stunning Kid.

"Well Danny, I'm back in the saddle again and I'm ready to go. I'll see you when I get back," reckoned Stephen as he rode out between the two huge boulders.

Stephen rode up the hill and down the hill where the road to Brownsville was. As he began riding towards Brownsville and away from Danny, he saw Danny following in the distance. After ten minutes into his ride, Danny disappeared.

Stephen rode ten minutes more. Now that he was sure that Danny wasn't following him anymore, Stephen rode behind some large bushes next to the road and pulled the two way radio out of his saddle bags.

Chapter 52

CALLING REX

"Hello Rex. Rex can you hear me? This is Stephen calling, over"

"I hear you," answered Rex. "I was beginning to worry about you. It's been five days since you walked out on that Homesteader's Meeting. What have you got for me? Over."

"Right now, I'm riding Thunder and I'm on my way to Brownsville to join Michael, The Magnificent and his gang," replied Stephen. "It turns out that Michael and Dean's gang are now working together. When this gang raided Twin Forks, Danny played the part of The Stunning Kid. Danny doesn't want to be The Stunning Kid anymore.

I think I really convinced Belle and Danny that I'm through being a U. S. Deputy Marshal because I lost Thunder. They also believe that you and I really got into it at the Homesteader's Meeting. Because of that, they gave me the job of being The Stunning Kid as part of the gang. How is Hannibal and Scooter taking it after what I did to them? Over."

"Scooter knows there is something wrong. He's not mad at you. He just wants you to come back," explained Rex. "Hannibal hasn't got over the fact that you hit him and knocked him to the floor. It even bothers him more that you talked to Scooter the way you did, over."

"I know how they must feel. It really hurt me to do that to them, especially since they are my best friends," sighed Stephen. "When I saw Hannibal on the floor after I knocked him down, I felt really bad and had to leave, over."

"I know it was very hard for you to do that," insisted Rex. "It had to be done for you to get into the gang. It was the only way I knew how to get Thunder back and catch up to this gang of thieves and cutthroats at the same time.

When this is all over, Columbo and I will get Hannibal and Scooter to forgive you for what you did to them, because it was in the line of duty. You need to forgive yourself as well, over."

"Here's what you need to do next," instructed Stephen. "Arrest Belle, Danny and Belle's bartender, Eddie. It might even be a good idea to arrest everybody who works in the saloon and shut it down. I don't want to take a chance that Michael will find out what's going on with me joining the gang and then end up riding into a trap.

Their hideout is north of Dodge where we meant up with Belle and Eddie while we were looking for Thunder. Have Eddie or Danny take you to the hideout right away.

There is an old prospector that has been tied up in their cabin for the last four days without food and water. He's about done for. You'll need to get in touch with Dr. Genesis to take care of the old prospector. When you bring the prospector back to Dodge, bring Lightning with you, over."

"When are you going to get back to me after you reach Brownsville?" questioned Rex. "Over."

"I would suggest that you have Columbo and his squad go to the hide out and you follow me to Brownsville with your squad," replied Stephen. "Don't come into Brownsville. Just stay in range with the two way radios in case I need you. After Columbo finishes his job, he can follow you to Brownsville, over."

"Who's going to take care of the prisoners while we're gone?" asked Rex. "Over."

"Ask Sheriff Gold to send a couple of his Deputies to Dodge. Oliver and the Deputies can watch the prisoners and Dodge. The homesteaders will always help if you need them," explained Stephen. "Ask Hannibal if he would like to ride Lightning when he comes to Brownsville, over and out."

Chapter 53

Stephen And Michael

It is now 6:00 p. m. in Brownsville and Stephen is setting at a table in the corner of the saloon sipping on a beer. As the clock strikes 6:01 p. m., Michael walks through the door of the saloon.

"Hello Stephen," greeted Michael. "I'm very glad to see you. I really have been wanting to talk to you, since I saw you last as The Great Stunning Kid. I still owe you for saving my life when you found me alongside of the road."

"You don't owe me anything," replied Stephen. "I would have done that for anybody. That's one of my codes in life to always help others in need. When I saw you laying alongside of the road, I just couldn't ride away because I had no choice but to help you. If I had to do it over again, I still would be there for you."

"I know you would. If you had been laying there alongside of the road and I found you, I would have left you to die, because I just don't like people," explained Michael. "Even though you saved my life, I did the opposite to you by trying to hurt and destroy you're reputation as The Stunning Kid and it was the wrong choice.

Let me explain. Belle sent me a telegram, hiring me to do a job for her. She was going to pay me $2,000.00. She sent me a $1,000.00 in advance and was going to pay me the other $1,000.00 when I finished the job.

Believe me. When you helped me, I didn't know what the job was. I don't like people and if I had to hurt them, I really didn't care.

It wasn't until I got to Dodge and talked to Belle that I found out that she wanted me to get rid of you. I told her that I couldn't because I felt indebted to you and even though I am a badman I always pay my debts.

Since I accepted the $1,000.00 in advance, Belle made me keep my deal with her. I couldn't make her change her mind. One thing led to another and I took over her gang. Now with my gang and Belle's Gang there are fourteen of us plus Belle.

When Dean Dickerson bought your black stallion from the stable hand, all of us was surprised to find The Stunning Kid outfit was with all that gear. That was just what we were looking for. I wanted one of us to portray The Stunning Kid with a gang of his own, to rob and terrorize everybody. Because my plan was to hurt you by giving you a bad reputation. I owed you and I didn't want to kill you. I just wanted to give The Stunning Kid a bad name so nobody would ever trust him again. Not only was we giving you a bad name, the gang was making some serious money when we raided the town of Twin Forks.

Danny took on the job of being The Stunning Kid and he was very good at it."

"That may be," replied Stephen. "I don't know if you know it, but Danny doesn't want to be The Stunning Kid anymore. When Belle was convinced I didn't want to be a U. S. Marshal anymore and all I wanted was to get my horse back, she offered me the job. I wasn't planning on being a badman, but here I am. Did Belle ever give you the other $1,000.00 she owed you?"

"No she never did. Thanks for reminding me. You have a good head on your shoulders," laughed Michael. "Belle made me stick to my deal with her and now it's time to collect from her. Not only will I make $2,000.00 from Belle, I also have her gang along with mine. With you, it makes fifteen of us and Belle."

"Now that you and I said what's on our minds, I want to know what's next for me?" asked Stephen. "Now that I'm part of the gang, do I call you Michael or boss?"

"No my friend. Just call me Michael. To answer your other question, I would like to tell you what my plans are. Right now, I don't know where you're going to fit in.

First of all, the way I plan our jobs is with strategy and execution. I'm always successful when I do that. The first two jobs was the one I told you about in the raid we made in Twin Forks. The second job we did as a new formed gang, was to hold up a stage coach with Danny as The Stunning Kid and his gang.

My next part of the plan was to bring my gang to Brownsville for a three day rest while Danny remained in Dodge. The idea was for the law to keep looking for The Stunning Kid and because he disappeared, they won't find him.

I have a friend who runs a trading post with the Indians a few miles west of Brownsville. His name is Big Jim Brady. I made a deal with him to combine his gang of twenty men with mine and rustle cattle as Indians. Big Jim is also able to supply the costumes to make us all look like Indians.

Chief Black Eagle's Tribe lives in the Black Water Canyon. Big Jim wants that land and he is willing to start an Indian War to get it. Today was our first raid as Indians on Bill Elliot's Ranch. We rustled his cattle and then left the right kind of evidence that would give Black Eagle's Tribe the blame."

"That is real intelligent thinking," reasoned Stephen. "No wonder The Marshals can't find you or The Stunning Kid."

"We all know that you used to be a Deputy Marshal," insisted Michael. "I can't trust you completely and I'm going to have Lefty keep you company at all times. I don't want to take a chance of you telegraphing The Marshals about our plans."

"If it will make you feel better, I give you my word that I will not send The Marshals a telegram about anything you told me," promised Stephen.

"I never promised I wouldn't call The Marshals on my two way radio," Stephen said to himself. "Michael, what I would like to know is how you get to Black Eagle's Camp?"

"I'll take you at your word about the telegram," answered Michael. "Now to get to Black Eagle's Camp, take the road on the other side of Bearcat until you get to The Black Fork Road. Take the left fork and it will take you to The Black Water Canyon where his camp is.

Its a good thing you made it to Brownsville today. Now that your here and you've joined our gang, we can use you to participate in our raid Thursday. According to Big Jim Brady, there is an Indian who is called Black Feather that has a cattle ranch just north of Bearcat. He is a member of Black Eagle's Tribe who provides the Indians with the meat they need to survive. Several members of the tribe help Black Feather with his cattle ranch.

It just goes against what Big Jim believes about an Indian being a cattle rancher. The day after tomorrow we're going to rustle all of his cattle as Indians. Big Jim hopes that will start The Indian War. Instead of being The Stunning Kid, you're going to be an Indian. How do you feel about that?"

"That will be very different than what I have been doing," explained Stephen. "It will be different because I always like to work alone. That reminds me. Have you ever heard of the Indian that tried to get a room without a reservation?"

"No, what happened to the Indian that tried to get a room without a reservation?" asked Michael. "Did the Indian get a room?"

"It's a joke. Don't you get it?" asked Michael.

"Oh yeah. I get it, I think," reasoned Michael. "Now to get back to the raid. We're going to get an early start by being at Buffalo Valley where Black Feather's herd is kept. We have to ride straight in because there are hills on three sides of the valley. Our horses can go up and down the hills, but the cattle won't even try. Since today is Tuesday, be ready to leave Brownsville Thursday morning at 6:00 a. m. We are to meet in front of this saloon. Any questions?"

"Where do I get my outfit to be an Indian?" asked Stephen.

"Big Jim will have everything you need when we get to Buffalo Valley," answered Michael.

"I'm sure that everybody in The Dean Dickerson gang has it in for me, especially Ace," insisted Stephen. "What guarantee do I have that I won't get shot in the back by one of the gang members?"

"You have my guarantee. Every one of them knows I owe you for saving my life. If they even say a cross word to you, they will have to answer to me, because I mean business," promised Michael.

"It's getting late and I want to go to the livery stable to take care of Thunder and spend some time with him. Where is Lefty?" asked Stephen. "Does he have to go with me?"

"You don't need Lefty to spend some time with your horse," reckoned Michael. "Go! go! Lefty isn't even back in Brownsville at the moment. Go to your horse."

"Thanks Michael. I'll see you in the morning," laughed Stephen as he left the saloon.

Chapter 54

MARSHAL REX TARILLO, WHERE ARE YOU?

A couple minutes later Stephen was in the stall with Thunder.

"Hello boy, did you miss me?" Stephen went on to say. "It looks like you and I have a lot of work to do. Right now, I better get you saddled so I can find someplace away from everybody and call Rex. After I talk to Rex, I'll bring you back to your stall. I will feed you and get you settled for the night."

Stephen immediately began to saddle Thunder and a couple minutes later he was in the saddle riding out of town where he found an isolated area hidden from the road, behind some trees and stopped. He reached into his saddle bags for his two way radio and started calling Rex.

"Rex, Rex, where are you?" asked Stephen. "Over."

"I'm here," answered Rex. "My squad and I are about three miles south of Brownsville. What have you got for me, over?"

"I just finished talking to Michael, The Magnificent about a half hour ago," explained Stephen. "He spilled everything to me. What he's done with the gang and what he plans to do and why. We have him now," Stephen continued to say as he told Rex everything Michael told him.

"Columbo and his squad are here. Since today is Tuesday and Michael is not going to rustle Black Feather's cattle until Thursday Morning, that will be plenty of time to set a trap for Michael and his little Indians.

I already have a plan to catch Michael at Buffalo Valley. I'm sure that Bill Elliot and Black Feather will be anxious to help me scalp a few Indians after they hear my plan. Tomorrow I'm going to go talk to Bill Elliot and send Columbo to talk to Black Feather about planning a surprise party for Michael, over."

"Right now, Michael doesn't suspect anything," reckoned Stephen. "I gave Michael my word that I wouldn't send you any telegrams about his gang. I never said anything about the two way radio. He would never figure out what I was talking about anyway. I better get Thunder back to the stable before Michael gets any ideas about me, over."

"OK Stephen, you be very careful. What you tell me about Michael, he is very smart, but dangerous," replied Rex. "Call me when you can. The ball is in my court and now it's time for Columbo and me to spring into action. I don't know what movie I heard that from, but I like the sound of it. Talk to you later, over"

"Don't worry, I'll be careful, very careful," answered Stephen. "As Scooter might say, see you later alligator. Just watch out for the crocodiles. Over."

"I heard that," yelled Scooter as he listened on his radio. "Be careful and don't do anything stupid. Over."

"Thanks for the advice. I won't do anything stupid," promised Stephen. "Over."

"You better take care of yourself!" yelled Hannibal. "I want you back safe and sound because I still owe you for knocking me on the floor. Over."

"I'm sorry I had to do that," replied Stephen. "It hurt me more to do that to you than the punch I gave you. I miss all of you guys and I'm anxious to see you. I'm going to follow your advice and get back to the stable. I'll see all of you on Thursday. Out."

Chapter 55

PLANNING THE TRAP

"Well, did everybody here that?" asked Rex.

"We sure did," answered Because. "Do you know what you are your planning to do next?"

"I definitely know what I'm going to do next," replied Rex. "This whole thing is getting interesting because I'm going to do something else that I've seen in the western movies. First, I'm going to draw a map in the dirt with a stick like they do in the westerns. The plan I have to catch this gang will be something else I saw in the movies. So, everybody gather around."

"I found a stick for you Rex. Will this work?" asked I'm Not Sure. "I asked I Don't Know if it would work. He didn't know and I wasn't sure, so I'm asking you?"

"Y ah, that will work just fine," answered Rex. "Now everybody gather round," instructed Rex as he drew a large upside down U in the dirt. "If Michael and his men want to be Indians, we will draw them into a trap Indian Style.

This is called Buffalo Valley. It is surrounded by three large hills which make up the large upside down U. Inside the U is Black Feather's cattle. I want Columbo's Squad on this side of the U and my squad on the opposite side. On the bottom part of the U, I want Bill Elliot and his men positioned. At the entrance of the U or valley, I want Black Feather's Men. I want all of us out of sight.

I want Michael and his men to be allowed to enter the valley as they planned. Once they get to the end of the valley or U, they will start to stampede the cattle. Black Feather's job will be to appear at that time and ride towards Michael's Indians with a few of his men ready to turn the cattle after they stampede. The rest of his men need to be shooting at Michael and his men. Michael and his men may stay and defend their ground after they stamped the cattle and they may think they only have Black Feather to fight.

That's when Columbo rides down the hill with his squad and I ride down the other hill with mine trapping Michael in a crossfire. Michael will then take his men over the bottom of the U or last hill to take cover and fight. That's where Bill Elliot's Men will be to greet Michael.

This time his strategy will be useless because he will be executed. We will have him, because he will be surrounded, trapped. How does that sound to everybody? Are there any questions?"

"I have a question Rex," inquired Scooter.

"OK Marshal, what's your question?" asked Rex.

"When do we eat?" asked Scooter.

"Go ask Happy. I'm sure he'll have something to eat for a growing boy like you," replied Rex.

"We have a day to plan our trap. Columbo, I want you to take your squad and go talk to Black Feather about Michael and our trap. I'm going to catch up with Bill Elliot. Columbo, after your done talking to Black Feather meet me at Buffalo Valley so we can complete my strategy and Michael's execution.

Make sure all of you get enough sleep, because I want to get an early start tomorrow. Scooter, you make sure you get enough to eat so I don't have to listen to you telling me how hungry you are all day long."

Chapter 56

THE TRAP

It is now 6:00 a. m. Thursday morning. Michael's gang is all sitting on their horses in front of the saloon waiting for Michael to give the order to ride out.

"So, you're the Great Stunning Kid," Ace said to Stephen. "I don't know how you was brought into our gang. Now that you're around me you better watch your step. The gang and I owe you for the trouble you caused us and making us walk to town without our boots and pants. It was very painful to walk over everything on the ground and very embarrassing to walk back through town with no pants on."

"I was a Deputy Marshal and that's what I was paid to do," explained Stephen. "Since you're a badman, I'm sure nobody will ever see you helping old ladies across the street. Now that I'm part of the gang, I will do the job I was hired to do.

Just don't get in my way. You know what I'm capable to do. The only way you can beat me is to shoot me in the back and if I'm not careful, that's probably what you intend on doing."

Riding up to Ace, Michael demanded, "Stephen is now part of our gang. Ace, don't you or anybody start trouble with Stephen, or you will have to deal with me, clear.

I just want everybody to do their job today without any slip ups. My strategy and execution won't be worth diddly squat if there are any problems between us. Now let's ride."

An hour later, Michael and Big Jim Brady's Men who are dressed as Indians arrive at the entrance of Buffalo Valley.

"Nobody is around. This is going to be easy pic-kens," reasoned Big Jim as he was talking to Michael. "There must be five hundred cattle in this herd. Black Eagle is going to start an Indian War after we rustle all his cattle. I'm sure of it.

Come on. Let's get on the other side of the cattle and start shooting to stampede them. If any of Black Feather's men get in our way, shoot them."

A couple minutes later, Big Jim and Michael's Men was on the other side of the cattle. As they looked out of the valley, they saw Black Feather and his men riding towards them.

"This is going to be like shooting fish in a barrel. This will start The Indian War I want. Let them have it," yelled Big Jim as Rex's men rode down the one side of The Buffalo Valley Hill and Columbo's men rode down the other side of the hill shooting with their 9 mm pistols at Michael's Indians.

"It's The Marshals. They're everywhere. They're everywhere. I don't know what kind of guns they have that are shooting all those bullets, but I'm getting out of here!" yelled Michael as he and the gang rode toward the hill where Bill Eliot and his men greeted them with their Winchester rifles.

"So much for your strategy and execution!" screamed Ace as he pointed his gun at Michael, shooting him off his horse. Looking at the hill that Rex's men rode down, Ace began to escape, by riding up the hill.

"He's mine!" shouted Scooter to Stephen as he began to go after Ace.

After Ace rode a ways on the top of the hill, he saw Scooter coming up right behind him on Mischief. Ace then stopped his horse and climbed down.

"So, Marshal, you think your tough enough to capture me," bragged Ace as Scooter rode up behind him. "Get off your donkey and let's have our hoopty do."

Not answering Ace, Scooter jumped off of Mischief and walked over to Ace and began to shiver.

"It's true. You are tougher than you look," cried Ace as fear began to set in.

As Ace froze in his tracks, Scooter walked up to Ace taking a jab at him, followed by a right cross finished with a left hook overhand right combination and Ace fell to the ground unconscious.

Following Scooter, Stephen saw the fight as he approached the pair of fighters.

"You did it Scooter. You beat the Bare Handed Champion of Boxing and you didn't even need Wyatt Earp to referee," reasoned Stephen as he began to hear Don from the 21st century talking to him.

"Stephen, I can't bring you home! I can't bring you home! My German Shepard jumped on top of the time machine, knocking it over! I can't fix it!" roared Don. "I can't fix it! I can't fix it!"

Believing he was stuck in time, Stephen began to wake up. Stephen fell asleep while he was watching the western channel.

"What a relief. That was quite a dream I had," said Stephen to himself. "I can hardly wait to tell Rex, Hannibal, Scooter and the rest of the gang about my dream."

It was now daylight and time for Stephen to get ready to go to work.

About the Author

David, who is the author retired after working thirty-five years at Ralston Purina. David got a two-year degree from Scott Community College in 1992 for General Studies. He was a newsletter editor for The Dad's Club, his church and The Junior Chamber of Commerce over the years. He coached Dad's Softball for thirty years. He always taught the kids that played for him that life is like a sport, which encouraged him to write his other three books, "Life Is Too Short", Life Is Too Short: Choices In Life" and "Life Is Too Short: Life Is What We Make It". David would joke around once in a while about writing a short story about a Dwarf going around robbing and killing people. He was caught by the police and this Dwarf was sentenced to the electric chair by a judge. David was going to call this short story, Small Fry. A friend of his suggested he write a book about Small Fry. After thinking about it, David came up with a more detailed version of Small Fry and all the Danger, Excitement and Adventure is in this book.

In David's second book in this series, the Danger, Excitement and Adventure continues as The West Side Kids team up with Stunning Stephen Edwards in Stunning Stephen Edwards and The West Side Kids in The Invisible Man. This story has a real live boxer mixed in the world of fiction containing The West Side Kids, two Davenport Police Detectives and The Jerry Dickerson Gang. There is no violence, but lots of laughs. The story line will make the reader want to keep on reading to find out what happens next. Oh yeah.

Now this third book of the series continues as the boys travel in time with The Adventures Of Stunning Stephen Edwards as The Stunning Kid in The Time Traveling Marshals.

Partner, you and I have all have heard about the heroes of the old west. Now a new mysterious hero is on the horizon known as The Stunning Kid riding Thunder, who fights for justice in Dodge City Kansas, 1880. When he is not The Stunning Kid, he becomes Stephen Edwards, Deputy Marshal riding Lightning. A storm is brewing as Stunning Stephen Edwards saddles up Thunder and Lightning to challenge The Dean Dickerson Gang.

Printed in the United States
By Bookmasters